NEW RECRUIT

CONFIDENTIAL

COBRA FILES

Case no. 3-15-2-18-1-19/1-18-5/6-15-18-5-22-5-18

Operation: Scared Dog and
Shiny Stones

Details: An intriguing case of

dognappers and diamond thieves

Status: **TOP SECRET**

D0306573

For my Mum and Dad

OXFORD
UNIVERSITY PRESS

Great Clarendon Street, Oxford OX2 6DP

Oxford University Press is a department of the University of Oxford.
It furthers the University's objective of excellence in research, scholarship,
and education by publishing worldwide. Oxford is a registered trade mark
of Oxford University Press in the UK and in certain other countries

Copyright © Anne Miller 2020
Illustrations copyright © Becka Moor 2020

The moral rights of the author/illustrator have been asserted
Database right Oxford University Press (maker)

First published 2020

All rights reserved. No part of this publication may be reproduced,
stored in a retrieval system, or transmitted, in any form or by any means,
without the prior permission in writing of Oxford University Press,
or as expressly permitted by law, or under terms agreed with the appropriate
reprographics rights organization. Enquiries concerning reproduction outside
the scope of the above should be sent to the Rights Department, Oxford
University Press, at the address above

You must not circulate this book in any other binding or cover
and you must impose this same condition on any acquirer

British Library Cataloguing in Publication Data

Data available

ISBN: 978-0-19-277363-0

1 3 5 7 9 10 8 6 4 2

Printed in India

Paper used in the production of this book is a natural,
recyclable product made from wood grown in sustainable forests.
The manufacturing process conforms to the environmental
regulations of the country of origin.

London Borough of Richmond Upon Thames	
RTTE DISCARDED	
90710 000 426 356	
Askews & Holts	
JF	£6.99
	9780192773630

MICKEY

-- AND THE --

ANIMAL SPIES

ANNE MILLER

Illustrated by
BECKA MOOR

OXFORD
UNIVERSITY PRESS

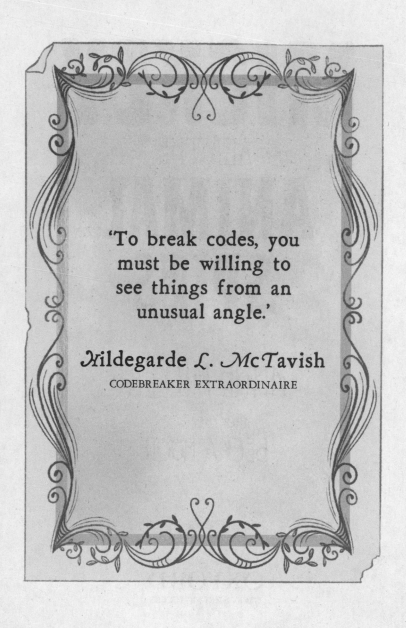

'To break codes, you
must be willing to
see things from an
unusual angle.'

Hildegarde L. McTavish

CODEBREAKER EXTRAORDINAIRE

Chapter 1

It was a Friday after school and Mickey was hanging at an unusual angle, her hair almost brushing the floor beneath her as she tried to take even breaths.

'And that's time— everyone come back up,' came the firm voice of her gymnastics teacher.

'Thank you,' Mickey whispered under her breath as she slowly put herself the right way up. The truth was that Mickey was not a natural athlete. She was much more likely to be found sitting in the shade with a book than doing anything that involved physical activity. But at the beginning of the year she had marched up to the school clubs' noticeboard and signed herself up to a weekly gymnastics class. And it was all because of codes.

Mickey really loved codes. More than cartoons, more than ice cream—not quite more than her parents, but it was definitely close. She cracked puzzles over her cornflakes in the morning, made up new ones as she went about her day, and solved them while she slept.

Her favourite was **Morse code**—all those dots and dashes that could be sent by tapping a wall or flashing a torch. But she also loved the **Caesar cipher**—where you move the letters on a few places then work out how far they've travelled. And she'd recently discovered a pile of **naval flags** in a cupboard at school—they looked like bunting for a school fête, but actually each flag was a coded message that could be understood across languages and countries around the world.

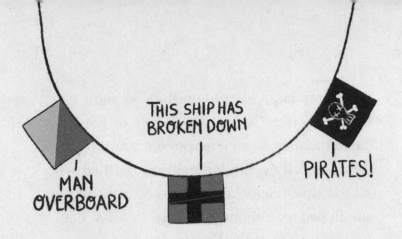

THIS SHIP HAS
BROKEN DOWN

MAN
OVERBOARD

PIRATES!

So that was why Mickey had dedicated
every Friday after school to gymnastics,
because, in the words of her hero,
Hildegarde L. McTavish,
legendary codebreaker and spy extraordinaire:
**'To break codes, you must be willing to
see things from an unusual angle.'**
What better way to see things from a new
angle than while hanging upside down from
a balance beam?

Of course, Mickey hadn't actually found
any hidden codes to crack yet, but she knew
each day brought fresh opportunities for
mystery solving, and she did her best to be
prepared for any eventuality. As such, there
were two books she always carried with her:

a battered copy of Hildegarde's memoir **Cracking the Codes**, which told of her daring career as a codebreaker, and Mickey's own carefully compiled code book filled with all the tips, tricks, and pieces of information she hoped would one day help to solve her first ever case. At the front of her book, Mickey had written out her own three key rules of codebreaking:

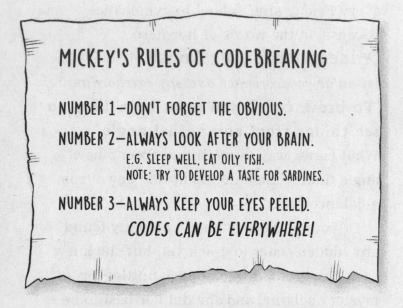

MICKEY'S RULES OF CODEBREAKING

NUMBER 1—DON'T FORGET THE OBVIOUS.

NUMBER 2—ALWAYS LOOK AFTER YOUR BRAIN.
E.G. SLEEP WELL, EAT OILY FISH.
NOTE: TRY TO DEVELOP A TASTE FOR SARDINES.

NUMBER 3—ALWAYS KEEP YOUR EYES PEELED.
CODES CAN BE EVERYWHERE!

It was rule number 3 that would change Mickey's life that very afternoon . . .

Chapter

As always on a Friday afternoon, Rachel
Downstairs had picked up Mickey from
gymnastics on her own way home to the block
of flats they both lived in. They were sitting
side by side on the bus, and Mickey was
craning her neck as she tried to read
(and answer) Rachel's homework over
her shoulder as they bumped their
way through the city's winding roads.

'It's a "K",' she piped up.

Rachel looked up from her worksheet.
'What is?'

'The chemical symbol for
potassium. It sounds like it should
be a 'p' but it isn't.'

Mickey loved science. One
of her best school trips was the
time they all went
to a science fair and got to

9

try out lots of experiments.
Ben Campbell had been asked
to touch a thing called a
'Van de Graaff generator'
that gives off a static charge.
It made all his long hair stand
on end, which Mickey had
thought was quite a bold look.

'Thanks,' Rachel said, writing the answer
in with her purple pen. 'Haven't you got any
homework?'

Mickey shook her head. 'But I could
practise my codes.'

Rachel waved distractedly. 'Well that
should keep you busy.'

Mickey liked Rachel a lot, but she didn't
really understand about the importance of
codes. Mickey tried looking out of the window
(because of rule number 3), but they were in
a lot of traffic and her window was currently
completely taken up by the side of a huge
lorry. She switched her gaze to the inside of
the bus—looking for anything surprising—
and saw a poster at the front of the bus for

a storage company, which had a large red squirrel as its logo. There was a boy standing next to it with a huge musical instrument case that was almost as big as he was. Then, as she looked up, something very odd caught her eye. A piece of paper had been stuck to the bus, above the window on her left.

Mickey felt as if someone had squeezed her stomach, the way you'd wring out a sponge . . .

It was a
code!

8-5-12-16 23-1-14-20-5-4!
3-1-14 25-15-21
3-18-1-3-11 3-15-4-5-19?
FMFWFO LJOH TUSFFU-1

She looked around the bus again but no one else seemed to have noticed it. Instead they were all looking down at their feet, or looking at their phones, which meant this code was hiding perfectly in plain sight!

Mickey quickly pulled out her notebook and copied out the code. She could feel the blood pumping in her brain because she knew what the first line said already. It was a number substitution (where each number represented the appropriate letter in the alphabet), and it said '**HELP WANTED!**' SOMEBODY NEEDED HER HELP.

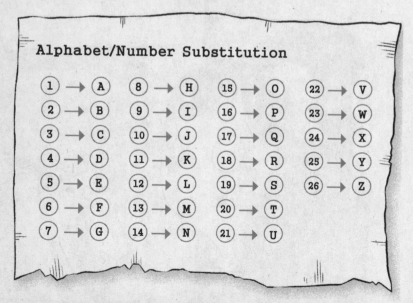

Alphabet/Number Substitution

1 → A	8 → H	15 → O	22 → V
2 → B	9 → I	16 → P	23 → W
3 → C	10 → J	17 → Q	24 → X
4 → D	11 → K	18 → R	25 → Y
5 → E	12 → L	19 → S	26 → Z
6 → F	13 → M	20 → T	
7 → G	14 → N	21 → U	

Mickey was about to tackle the next line when the bus arrived at their stop and Rachel Downstairs insisted they both get off. The rest of the puzzle would have to wait until they got back to their block of flats. Mickey hopped off the bus, and in her hurry nearly tripped over a black cat that was sitting in the middle of the pavement.

'Sorry!' she said breathlessly to the cat. Is a black cat crossing your path good luck or bad luck? Mickey couldn't remember as she raced home to solve the rest of the code.

Once inside, Mickey ran straight to the desk in the corner of her bedroom. She copied the code on to a big piece of paper, stuck it to her noticeboard with a pin shaped like a ladybird, and then leaned back in her seat and stared at it.

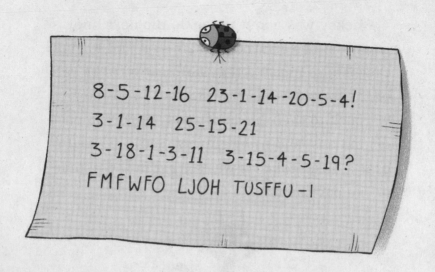

8-5-12-16 23-1-14-20-5-4!
3-1-14 25-15-21
3-18-1-3-11 3-15-4-5-19?
FMFWFO LJOH TUSFFU -1

This was Mickey's favourite way of cracking codes: staring.

But like a swan gliding calmly across a lake while paddling furiously under the water, Mickey's eyes were still but her brain was working at top speed.

The code for the second line was the same as the first. So the numbers **3–1–14 25–15–21 3–18–1–3–11 3–15–4–5–19** became: '**Can you crack codes?**'

'YES!' Mickey cried. Yes, she definitely could.

Mickey wondered how many other people

might have got this far—lots of people must have been near the poster but not everybody looked up. Sometimes Mickey thought you could sit on the bus in fancy dress and no one would even notice unless you accidentally stepped on their toes.

The next line of code **FMFWFO LJOH TUSFFU −I** was much harder. Mickey stared, blinked her eyes, and stared again, but the key refused to spring to her mind.

She rubbed her eyes and glanced at the clock just as she heard a key turning in the lock and then a familiar voice.

'Mickey, love, I'm home.' Her dad was back from work. He was bound to come in any minute and ask about her day. Mickey was almost tempted to show him the code but felt like she was very nearly there herself. Hildegarde certainly wouldn't have given up so easily. And success came through perseverance. Reluctantly, she covered up the code with a book. The last line, and the missing piece of the puzzle, would have to wait.

'FROGS!' Mickey yelled out loud the next morning, startling herself awake. She had been having a very strange dream where she was jumping backwards and forwards on giant lily pads. Just as she missed one and was about to land in the cold water, her brain had shaken her awake, reminding her that she wasn't in fact a frog. She was a human. In her bed. Not the water.

As she enjoyed the warmth of being on dry land, something in her brain clicked and she wondered if the trick to the puzzle was moving the letters backwards or forwards.

Sensing the excitement of a solution in sight, Mickey sprang out of bed (no need to hang upside down today) and ran over to the code pinned to the wall. She grabbed a pencil from the pot and started scribbling in her notebook. What if the last two symbols weren't letters but were an instruction to MINUS ONE?

FMFWFO LJOH TUSFFU−I

Working her way through the code Mickey moved all the letters back one place and to her delight found that the code started to make sense.

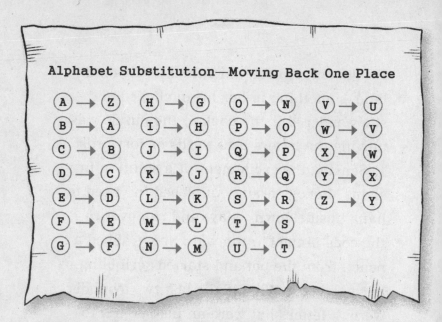

Alphabet Substitution—Moving Back One Place

A → Z H → G O → N V → U
B → A I → H P → O W → V
C → B J → I Q → P X → W
D → C K → J R → Q Y → X
E → D L → K S → R Z → Y
F → E M → L T → S
G → F N → M U → T

F M F W F O   L J O H
E L E V E N   K I N G

T U S F F U
S T R E E T

In fact, it didn't just make sense, it spelled out an address, Eleven King Street.

HELP WANTED!
Can you crack codes?
Eleven King Street

It made sense! Mickey felt a huge grin spread across her face, and she leapt to her feet triumphantly. She then realized there was nobody else in the room, and as she'd been keeping the code a secret there was no one to share her success with. Instead she gave a smart nod to Hildegarde, who was smiling out at her from the cover of her book, and she sat back down to work out the Next Steps.

There was a King Street near her house— and while Mickey's logical brain realized it would be a coincidence of huge proportions if it was the same one, her code-loving heart kept whispering, 'But what if it is?' The puzzle had asked for help, and Mickey knew she must at least try. *Someone* needed to find the solution, so why shouldn't it be her?

It was a Saturday, so Mickey headed straight to the kitchen where her parents were making breakfast. She hoped they weren't going to suggest eating some of her tins of sardines that were still cluttering up the cupboards. She was still waiting for the memory of last week's sardine pizza to fade away.

'Can we go to King Street today?' she asked,

trying to keep her tone of voice casual.

Her dad looked up from where he was buttering toast. 'Why do you want to go there?'

'We thought we might meet up with your cousins today,' said her mum, wrapping her hands around her morning cup of tea. Mickey saw a tin of sardines sitting ominously next to the kettle.

'But this is really important,' insisted Mickey.

'Why?' her mum asked.

Mickey realized she had three options:

① explain to her parents about the code on the bus. But they might not let her explore King Street.

② visit her cousins instead and forget about the code. As soon as she thought this, she knew this wasn't an option either.

③ go to King Street at the earliest opportunity. Mickey knew this is exactly what Hildegarde would do, and so it was what she would do too. After all, why should she have to wait until she was grown up to be a brave codebreaker when there was an opportunity right here?

She decided then that she would be taking herself to King Street as soon as possible.

After breakfast, Mickey remembered her mum had wanted to go to the supermarket, so she waited until she had set off, then watched her dad settle down next to the radio, knowing it wouldn't be long before he dozed off.

She was just going to have a quick look
at King Street so would probably be back
before either of them realized she was gone,
but just in case they worried, Mickey left
a note saying she had nipped into town.
She hovered in the hall until she heard her
dad snoring and then slipped back to her
room, got dressed quickly, checked that both
Hildegarde's book and her code book were
safely stowed in her backpack, then picked
up her dad's umbrella in case it rained. Heart
beating fast, Mickey tiptoed out of the flat.

The umbrella was a very pleasing size to hold and made a smart tapping sound as she prodded the ground on the walk over to King Street, making her feel as if something magical might just happen.

King Street was a very normal-looking street. Mickey walked down it, tapping her umbrella, the taps getting faster as she passed numbers **5**, **7**, and **9**. But then she came to number **13** and stopped. Numbers **9** and **13** were big beige office blocks, but where was number **11**? She retraced her steps and spotted a very narrow path between the two buildings. She wandered down the path and spotted a small sign that said 'Eleven' attached to the door of what looked like a garden shed.

Mickey carefully looked around her. Could this be right? She gripped the umbrella and knocked on the door. There was no answer.

She tried again. Still nothing.

She gently pushed the door and, to her surprise, it opened. She called out a tentative 'Hello?' as she stepped through.

The shed was empty aside from an old desk, right in the middle of the room. And on the desk, a glass tank containing a single solitary goldfish. Mickey's parents were always talking about the importance of tidying up, but she couldn't help thinking the owners of this shed had taken things a little too far—there wasn't even a tin of emergency biscuits anywhere, and that is something no room should be without.

Mickey felt a sinking feeling of disappointment that nothing was going to happen after all. She'd been so sure she'd cracked the code correctly, but this was just a shed.

'Eleven King Street,' she murmured under her breath. Where had she gone wrong?

Suddenly Mickey had that strange feeling you have when you can feel someone is looking at you. She looked around, but there was nobody else there. Nobody apart from the goldfish—who was staring straight at her.

And then something strange happened.

The goldfish tapped its head against its tank three times.

There was a peculiar grinding noise.

And then the wall behind the desk swung backwards.

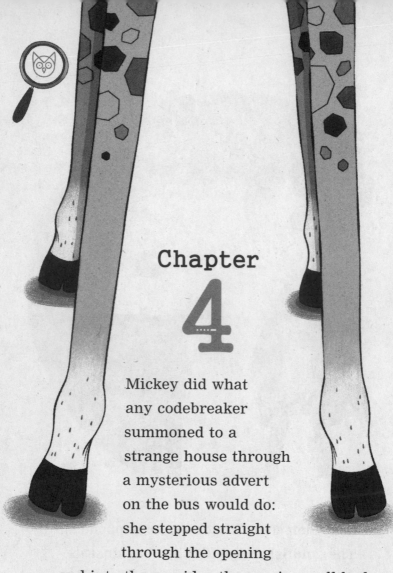

Chapter

4

Mickey did what
any codebreaker
summoned to a
strange house through
a mysterious advert
on the bus would do:
she stepped straight
through the opening
and into the corridor the moving wall had
just revealed. As she turned around to take
in the new room, she bumped into four tall
yellow-and-brown patterned poles.

Poles that on closer inspection were actually legs . . . the legs of a very tall giraffe wearing a bow tie.

Mickey's brain barely had a chance to work out what was happening because the giraffe immediately jumped into the air and let out an ear-piercing shriek.

'AAAAAAAARGH!'

Panicking, Mickey dived behind a nearby pot plant. She took a steadying breath, remembering rule number 2:

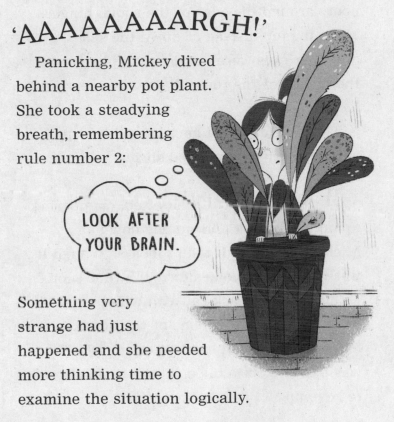

LOOK AFTER YOUR BRAIN.

Something very strange had just happened and she needed more thinking time to examine the situation logically.

She'd walked into a shed, containing a desk with a fish tank on a table. So far, so (relatively) normal. But then a secret door had swung open and on the other side—well . . .

Mickey peered round the side of the plant. There was a very tall desk, several doors around the edge of the room, hinged along the top instead of down the side, and—her eyes were not deceiving her—in the middle of the room there was a terrified-looking giraffe.

The giraffe caught her eye and let rip with another high-pitched shriek.

'**Eeeeeeek!**' it cried, clambering up on to the desk and staring down at Mickey in horror. It didn't look as though it was planning to come down any time soon.

Just then, a black cat with white paws came tearing through one of the doors, followed by a small, rather round rat who was hanging on to the cat's tail in an effort to keep up.

'Bertie, what is going on?' the cat demanded. 'Why are you sounding the alarm?'

'Hu-hu-hu-human!'

stuttered the giraffe, pointing a foot in Mickey's direction.

The cat let out an irritated sigh.

'There are no humans here, Bertie. You must have been daydreaming again. Honestly . . .' The cat sighed and looked over at the rat. 'He only got the guard job because of his height. We might have been better off with a mouse.'

'You're right, Clarke. A mouse would in fact do an excellent job. We rodents are excellent guards,' the rat replied. 'But I think something really has spooked old Bertie.'

The rat scanned the room with inquisitive eyes.

Mickey held her breath and tried to make herself as small as possible.

'How intriguing,' the rat murmured, scampering straight towards her hiding place. 'Who do we have here?'

In Mickey's attempt to keep a low profile, her brain had refused to process one key fact: these animals were *talking*. And she could understand what they were saying.

Suddenly, she felt woozy

and then

everything

went

black.

Chapter
5

Mickey felt a strange tickling feeling on her left hand, which drew her back to the real world. She tried to remember what had happened. Goldfish . . . giraffe . . . cat . . . rat . . . talking animals . . .

Animals which were still right in front of her, she realized as she looked over and saw the rat gently running back and forth across her hand.

'Oh good, you're back!' he said.

'How's the, um, giraffe doing?' she mumbled, trying to make her head stop spinning.

'Bertie? Perfectly fine. Or will be once he calms down,' the rat replied. 'He does have a tendency to panic, which isn't ideal for his position. Once we thought he was going to faint, so we tried to make him put his head between his knees to calm himself down, but he's got an awful lot of neck so he knocked himself out on the floor.'

'How did you get here?' the cat cut in, looking at Mickey suspiciously. 'You look familiar . . . '

'How . . . how are you able to talk?' asked Mickey.

'The same way you are,' the cat snapped rather rudely. 'Humans really don't pay much attention, do they?'

'I think what Clarke is saying,' interrupted the rat, 'is that while all humans appear familiar with the concept of talking to one another, they don't expect or notice animals doing the same. Of course, we try not to cause unnecessary alarm, but since we're in our own headquarters we feel we should be able to speak freely here.'

'*Your* headquarters,' repeated Mickey, slowly sitting up. 'Did *you* set the code?'

'Ah, the recruitment puzzle,' said the rat. 'Indeed. And you solved it? Well, that is quite the surprise. I wonder . . . '

'But you're only a small person,' the cat

interrupted, swishing its tail in annoyance.

'Clarke, you are not displaying correct manners towards our guest,' the rat said wearily. 'Perhaps we should start again. My name is Rupert, and this is Clarke.'

'I'm Mickey,' she replied.

'Well, we're very pleased to meet you, Mickey.'

The cat hissed. 'You *do* look familiar. This is the child who ran in to me yesterday! Clumsy as well as young. Hardly spy material.'

The rat looked apologetically at Mickey. 'We *are* pleased to meet you, but I think perhaps we should go and discuss this with Coby. We shall return soon.'

'Wait!' Mickey called after them. 'Who is Coby?'

'Coby?' Rupert called back over his shoulder. 'She's in charge.'

'And, what kind of animal is she?' asked Mickey, hoping Coby wouldn't be anything too scary.

Clarke turned round and looked Mickey straight in the eye. 'She's a cobra.'

Chapter

6

'A cobra?' Mickey double-checked when
Rupert came scuttling back into the room.
She'd read a book about cobras and knew they
could be up to six metres long, could smell
with their tongues, and had venomous fangs
that could stop a person's heartbeat.

'Yes, don't make any sharp movements
around her—but you'll be fine,' he said,
smiling up at her reassuringly. 'Now,
are you ready to meet her?'

Mickey firmly instructed
herself to be brave and nodded.

As Rupert gestured for
Mickey to follow him, she rose
to her feet unsteadily and made
her way through a door into a meeting
room. She hadn't been to many meetings
before—but she imagined there weren't many
like this.

Sitting around the table were a spider monkey, working her way through a plate of grapes, Clarke swishing his tail impatiently, and between them, a huge cobra who Mickey assumed was Coby. There was one empty seat with a sign that said 'Tilda' and another where the name had been crossed out, but Mickey could see the word 'Harry'.

'Where's the sloth?' Coby asked sharply.

'Tilda is running late. We'll have to start without her,' said the spider monkey with her mouth full of grapes.

'She's always late!' sighed Clarke.

Just then, the door swung open and a slightly bashful-looking sloth crawled in . . .

'Sorry, everyone. It's just quite a long walk,' she said.

Mickey watched as Tilda moved extremely slowly towards the table in the centre of the room. Eventually, she got to her chair, pulled it out, and climbed on to it—while Clarke fidgeted in his chair with annoyance.

Mickey gave a polite cough, and the cobra swivelled round in her chair to face her.

'I see our guest has arrived,' Coby hissed.

Everyone turned to stare at Mickey, who tried to stare back without looking too frightened.

'This is Mickey,' Coby continued. 'Rupert says she solved our recruitment puzzle.'

Tilda looked Mickey up and down. 'Weren't we hoping for one with a bit . . . more experience?'

'You're one to talk,' said Clarke, stroking his whiskers. 'Your specialist subject is sleeping. But you're right. She's too young to be a spy working for a top-secret organization like ours.'

'Quiet, Clarke,' said Coby, shifting her gaze to the spider monkey. 'Am I correct in thinking that you were in charge of placing

the advert, Astrid?'

'Yes indeed,' she replied eagerly.

'And on what basis did you make that decision?'

Astrid's face fell. 'The bus network carries lots of humans every day—it gave our advert the very best chance of being seen.'

'Yes, but also by *children*! Human cubs!' said Coby.

'Exactly,' added Clarke. 'Mickey is too young to have the skills required to join our team. You'll have to advertise again and get it right this time.'

Mickey suddenly found her voice. It was one thing to be summoned into a strange world of animal spies but quite another to find herself dismissed before she'd had a chance to prove herself.

'Excuse me,' she began politely. 'I'm here because I solved your code. If that is your recruitment test, doesn't that mean I passed?'

The cobra raised her head higher and tilted it to one side. 'The human makes a valid point. And she's here now, so it won't waste

too much time to create a brief file on her.
She may be useful when she grows up. Tilda,
take notes! Human, tell us what it is you do.'

'Um . . . mostly I go to school,' said Mickey,
who was quite indignant at being told she
couldn't be useful until she was grown up.
'My full name is Michaela Rose Thompson,
but everyone calls me Mickey . . . I'm very
good at codes and okay-but-improving at
gymnastics.'

Mickey looked around at the animals
seated at the table.

'And what is it *you* do?' she asked. 'If you
don't mind me asking?'

There was a hint of a smile on the snake's
face. 'Well, since as you rightly say you did
solve our recruitment puzzle, I see no harm
in giving you an
initial briefing . . .'

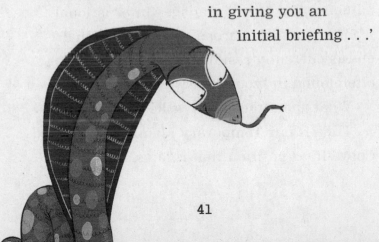

41

'My name is Coby. I am the head of **COBRA**, a secret animal organization founded by my great-grandparents to protect our country's animals in ways humans cannot even think of.

Sitting around this table are the members of the High Committee. Clarke manages Domestic Affairs—that's domesticated animals—or "pets"—as humans like to call them. Rupert manages Wild Affairs—that's free-roaming animals. And Astrid manages International Affairs—animals abroad and international guests currently residing within this country, often found in "zoos".'

'What about the sloth?' asked Mickey.

'Tilda is our Temporary Member,' explained Coby. 'It's a position that rotates among the other animals based on an animal-wide vote and, recently, in their wisdom, they decided it was time for a sloth to be on the committee.'

'And what a brilliant idea that was,' muttered Clarke sarcastically. Astrid threw a grape straight at his head.

'Ahem . . .' began Tilda, before letting her eyelids droop. Astrid gave her a sharp jab in the ribs and she jolted awake. 'I am here to represent the interests of animals that may be overlooked by our existing structure,' she continued, stifling a large yawn.

'We're a proud animal-led organization, but we've found it can be helpful to have a human onside,' continued Coby. 'Humans can do things we can't, like moving around without attracting suspicion. There are some places we just can't go—a spider monkey like Astrid would stand out quite a lot in an office or a bakery.'

'And people aren't always thrilled to see a rat in a restaurant,' added Rupert mournfully.

'And *you* have opposable thumbs,' Tilda nodded at Mickey.

'Yes, we're always foiled by that one,' said Coby. 'And we can't ask Astrid to do everything.' They all looked enviously at the spider monkey who gave them a thumbs up with her foot.

'Do you have any other humans working with you?' asked Mickey.

'Not at the moment . . .' said Astrid.

'We did . . . ' hissed Coby, her cool facade fading. 'We had a Human Liaison Officer named Harry. He seemed highly experienced and competent, but he went deep undercover and hasn't come back. We suspect he found the job too hard, but as our work is urgent we have been left with no choice but to try to recruit a more reliable human to fill his position.'

'And you think that's me?' Mickey asked, feeling a thrill of excitement.

'Not really,' said Coby swiftly. 'As I said, it is desirable that we get a fully-grown human with the knowledge and skills we need. We are dealing with a difficult case and have a code we can't crack. We suspect it requires

44

adult human knowledge.'

Mickey was starting to get annoyed. They already knew she was good at cracking codes. Why wouldn't they let her try?

'Will you at least let me have a look?' she asked.

'We should probably wait for a fully-grown human,' said Clarke dismissively.

Before she really knew what she was doing, Mickey turned to glare at the cat, her eyes blazing. 'You can't rule me out just because I'm not grown up yet. I've already solved your recruitment puzzle, I found my way to this HQ, and past the goldfish and the giraffe. If I told you that humans wouldn't think much of letting a cat solve a code, you'd think that was outrageous, so why do you think it's okay to do that to me? I can't do anything about my age, but I know what I'm good at and I'm good at codes.'

She turned to Coby and added, 'Give me a chance and I'll show you I'm just as good as any grown-up human.'

Clarke narrowed his eyes and opened his

mouth to say something rude but then seemed to think the better of it and sat back in his chair instead. 'I suppose it wouldn't hurt to try,' he said casually.

Coby nodded her approval. 'Very well,' she said. 'One of our field rats managed to intercept this message, but we don't know what it means.' She tapped a button with her tail and a message appeared on the wall above them.

'Can you do it?' Coby hissed.

Mickey gulped.

XOOO–OXO–OO–XO–XXO XX–O X–OOOO–O XOO–OO–OX–XX–XXX–XO–XOO–OOO

X–OOOO–O XXO–OXO–OX–XO–XOO OOOO–XXX–X–O–OXOO

OX–OOO–XOX OOXO–XXX–OXO XX–OO–OX

XXOOO–OXXO–XX OXXXX–OOOOX–X–OOOO OXXX–OOX–XO–O

Chapter

8

Mickey could feel the gazes of the **COBRA** members burning into her but forced herself to take her time. She leaned forwards in her seat, placed her chin in her hands, and stared at the code. Then, very slowly, she scanned it from left to right and then back again. Then she scanned up and down and criss-crossed, looking for anything that might reveal the key to solving the puzzle.

'**XOOO**,' she muttered softly. Somebody was either sending a lot of hugs and kisses, or it was a hidden message.

Mickey pulled out her code book and started scribbling down ideas.

'Have you got it yet?' asked Clarke, breaking her chain of thought.

'Give her a minute!' whispered Astrid. 'She's working.'

Mickey looked at her options—she didn't

know any puzzles that focused on Xs and Os—
apart from 'Noughts and Crosses', but that
was a game not a code. The main code she
knew that relied on two different symbols was
Morse code, but that was dots and dashes not
Xs and Os.

She drew a pattern of Os under the code
while she thought. Staring at them on their
own they looked a lot like dots—that was it!

'It's Morse code, but they've replaced the
dots with Os and the dashes with Xs,' Mickey
explained excitedly, as she began translating.

Morse code (with dots as Os and dashes as Xs)

A	OX	N	XO	0	XXXXX
B	XOOO	O	XXX	1	OXXXX
C	XOXO	P	OXXO	2	OOXXX
D	XOO	Q	XXOX	3	OOOXX
E	O	R	OXO	4	OOOOX
F	OOXO	S	OOO	5	OOOOO
G	XXO	T	X	6	XOOOO
H	OOOO	U	OOX	7	XXOOO
I	OO	V	OOOX	8	XXXOO
J	OXXX	W	OXX	9	XXXXO
K	XOX	X	XOOX		
L	OXOO	Y	XOXX		
M	XX	Z	XXOO		

'That's clever!' said Astrid.

'Well done, young Mickey!' said Rupert.

Mickey worked her way through the puzzle—changing the Xs and Os to dots and dashes and then finally into words that made sense:

BRING ME THE DIAMONDS
THE GRAND HOTEL
ASK FOR MIA
7 PM 14TH JUNE

'June 14th,' Mickey exclaimed. 'But that's next Saturday!'

'I'm impressed, small human,' said Coby. 'I suppose we could try you out on a trial basis. We need to crack the diamond case— you wouldn't believe what some humans get up to.'

Chapter

'Welcome to Operation Shiny Stones,' said
Coby dramatically. 'We've been tracking a
string of burglaries by a diamond thief. In
each case they have removed jewels from
homes containing high-profile pets. The thief
is still at large and our other members are
increasingly worried that their homes will be
targeted next.'

'The diamonds have all been taken
from incredibly wealthy humans. I am on
extremely good terms with their pets, being
a member of several private clubs myself,'
added Clarke, preening himself.

'Indeed,' said Coby. 'However, the strange
thing in this case is that these pets don't seem
particularly keen to help us. Without the trust
of the wider animal community, it is difficult
for us to operate. And, if they don't bring us
cases or assist us with our enquiries, then

our whole organization is at risk. Therefore, it is critical we find the humans responsible for the diamond thefts so we can swiftly bring the matter to an end and continue our usual work.'

Coby pressed a button and three photographs appeared on the wall. The first showed a cream-coloured cat with dark markings around the tips of her ears and her eyes—one of which was bright blue and one, dark green. The second photograph was of a very fluffy white and grey dog, and the third was the largest dog Mickey had ever seen.

'These are the animals whose homes the diamonds have been taken from: Ruby, a ragdoll cat, Max, an old English sheepdog, and Thor, a Leonberger dog. The most recent theft happened from Ruby's house. She lives with the footballer Alexi Holt on Eagle Gardens.'

'That's one of the most expensive streets in the city,' whispered Astrid.

'I go there all the time,' chipped in Clarke again. 'But unfortunately none of them have been able to help with our enquiries. '

'None of them saw or heard anything suspicious?' asked Mickey.

'If they did, they aren't telling us,' said Astrid.

Clarke hissed, 'We've been through this. They can't provide information they don't have!'

'So you've said,' said Coby. 'Mickey, despite the lack of cooperation, it is essential we solve this case to stop the thefts and prevent panic spreading further. The code you have just cracked could change everything. If the culprit is planning to acquire the diamonds at the hotel on Saturday, then we need to be there to intercept them.'

Suddenly there was the sound of scampering paws approaching. Coby paused to tilt her head to one side, and Astrid sprang to her feet, her tail poised for balance, on high alert.

The door flew open, and a beautiful golden spaniel came skidding into the room, fluffy ears flying behind him. He came to a shivering

stop right in front of the meeting table.

'I need your help. It's a matter of

LIFE AND DEATH.'

Chapter
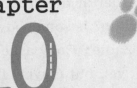

10

'Oh, not again, Winston,' groaned Clarke, displaying little sympathy for the trembling dog.

Astrid was already out of her seat and over at the dog's side. She rested a slim hand on top of his big fluffy paw in sympathy.

'Bertie said I could come straight th-th-through,' the spaniel stuttered.

'What is the problem this time, Winston?' said Clarke dismissively.

'It's my owner, Zadie. She's having a big party to celebrate her album launch next weekend, and I think she's in danger . . .' He paused to take a big gulp of air, and while doing so his gaze fell on Mickey. Winston's eyes widened with fear, and then he went very quiet and stared at the ground.

'Why might there be danger?' asked Astrid patiently. Winston shook his head and stared even harder at the ground.

'Winston? Is somebody threatening you or Zadie?' Coby asked.

'Not yet, but maybe! I need to keep her safe. She's my best friend!' Winston howled.

'Astrid,' said Coby. 'Take Winston for a walk and see if you can get him a bowl of water. Maybe he'll be able to tell us more once he's calmed down.'

As Astrid led Winston out of the room, the spaniel shot one more terrified glance at Mickey.

Once the door had swung shut behind them, Clarke turned to Coby.

'You're not taking this seriously, are you? I've kept a log of the various fears Winston's brought to my attention over the years. They include: the dark, waiting too long between meals, when it's too quiet, when it's too loud, not getting enough pats, getting too many pats, being stuck indoors, being stuck outdoors, being stuck in a cat flap, being dognapped—and now whatever this "unspecified danger" is.'

'He certainly seems distressed about

something. And given the recent diamond thefts and the fact that Winston's owner Zadie is an internationally famous pop star, there's every chance someone may be after him in order to get to her,' Coby announced. 'I hereby declare the launch of Operation Scared Dog and vow that **COBRA** will protect him.'

Though impressed by their quick response, Mickey couldn't help but be confused by Coby's approach to naming missions. The point of calling things 'Operation XXX' was so that anyone who overheard the phrase wouldn't know what you were talking about whereas 'Shiny Stones' and 'Scared Dog' didn't require too much skill to crack. She considered saying something, but Coby was in full flow, and she decided that sometimes the wisest thing to do was to stay quiet.

Just then the door swung open and Astrid popped her head back into the room. 'Yes?' asked Coby.

'One more piece of information you might be interested in,' Astrid called. 'Winston has just told me Zadie's album launch is on the 14th June and is at **The Grand Hotel**. That's the same time and place as the diamond drop.'

'Do you think they are connected?' asked Mickey. 'The diamond thief and the world-famous pop star in the same place at the same ime?'

There was a quiet moment while the other animals considered this possibility.

'Humans do the strangest things,' mused Clarke. 'Although it remains to be seen whether there is an actual threat to Winston and Zadie.'

'We can't take any risks,' said Coby. '**COBRA** will be present at **The Grand Hotel** next Saturday night and we will have two teams: one to provide protection for Winston— Clarke, I'd like you to take the lead there. And the other to investigate this diamond drop—Rupert, I'd like you and the rats to take charge of that. You can cover the ground much faster than the rest of us. Call in any extra help you can from your field operatives. There will be lots of humans to monitor and with two missions running at once we will need all the help we can get.'

'Can I come?' asked Mickey hopefully. It felt as though her whole life had been leading up to this moment.

'We can cover both missions effectively ourselves,' Clarke replied quickly.

Mickey, determined not to be left behind, placed her hands (with their opposable thumbs) on the table in front of her. 'But Coby said there were some things humans could do that you couldn't,' she said. 'Wouldn't it give both missions the best chance of success if I came too?'

'Fine,' said Coby. 'I suppose you will blend in and look less suspicious than Astrid, and less alarming than Rupert.' Mickey heard a loud sigh from Rupert's end of the table, but Coby carried on. 'You can help Clarke to maintain visual contact with Winston. Clarke will brief you.'

'If I must,' the cat replied, swishing his tail. 'Meet me here at 4 p.m. on June the fourteenth. And *don't* be late.'

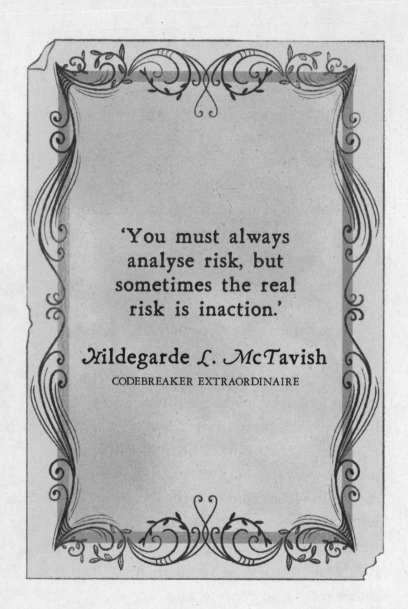

'You must always analyse risk, but sometimes the real risk is inaction.'

Hildegarde L. McTavish

CODEBREAKER EXTRAORDINAIRE

Chapter

In the days leading up to the mission, Mickey spent her time going over her spy notebook, and she spent every school break in the library, researching codes and famous secret agents throughout history.

Everyone at Mickey's school seemed more interested in running around and playing games than in methodically cracking mysteries, and it gave Mickey a nice warm feeling to think she finally had someone, or some animals, to talk to about her passion.

In the evenings, Mickey made sure to practise the secret **COBRA** identification code that Rupert had taught her. To ask an animal to confirm their **COBRA** identity, you tapped your head with your hand (or paw, tail, or wing if you had those instead). If an animal made the sign back to you, the correct response was to slowly blink your eyes three times (or to hide your eyes from view three times if the animal concerned couldn't blink).

When the day of the mission finally rolled around, Mickey sat through lunch with her parents, doing her best to act as though nothing unusual was about to happen. First her mum gave her a kiss and rushed out to work, and then her dad said he had some quiet work to do at the kitchen table. So Mickey polished off her dessert and casually told him she was going to watch a film at Rachel Downstairs's flat, which he said sounded like an excellent idea.

Back in her bedroom, Mickey brushed out her hair and tied it up again so she was ready for action. She carefully wiped the stray bits of mud off her laced up shoes and put on a fresh cardigan, giving it a shake to make herself look as smart as possible. Then, she packed and repacked her bag, making sure she had all of her Spy Essentials . . .

SPY ESSENTIALS

- CODE BOOK
- SUNGLASSES
- PHONE, COMPLETE WITH DIGITAL CAMERA (TO CAPTURE EVIDENCE), CALENDAR (TO SCHEDULE MISSIONS), AND MAPS (TO AVOID GETTING LOST)
- HANDKERCHIEF (TO AVOID THE DANGERS OF SNEEZING AT THE WRONG MOMENT)
- PLASTERS
- BASEBALL CAP (USEFUL IF YOU NEED TO HIDE YOUR FACE)
- TORCH
- A SMALL WALLET CONTAINING MONEY AND A SMALL MIRROR
- SANDWICH BAGS (TO USE AS EVIDENCE BAGS)
- SNACKS INCLUDING A HANDFUL OF SHERBET LEMONS

Mickey swung the bag over her shoulders and then tiptoed out of the door, her heart thumping with excitement.

Chapter

12

Mickey had heard that goldfish don't have very good memories so was pleasantly surprised when the fish recognized her and did the head-tapping trick as soon as she entered the shed. Mickey made her way through to the meeting room where she found the members of **COBRA** in the middle of a heated argument.

'I think you're making a terrible mistake. She's only a child!' she heard Clarke's voice proclaiming.

'We have been through this numerous times. Look at the seal above the door,' hissed Coby.

Clarke flicked his eyes to the portrait of the seal displayed above the door.

'Lord Sealingford of Seahouses. And your point is?' he asked.

'No. Look at the **COBRA** insignia above that. What kind of animal do you see in our logo?' came Coby's dangerous voice.

'A cobra,' Clarke muttered.

'Correct. This organization is not called CAT, it is called **COBRA**. Mickey is to be given a chance to prove herself, and my word will be respected.'

'Yes, Coby,' the cat replied through gritted teeth.

There was a short pause before the snake spoke again. 'I believe our human is here. Mickey, do come in.'

Nervously, Mickey, who had been hovering in the doorway, entered the room. She quickly tapped her head with her hand and was pleased to see Coby blink back at her three times.

'We don't need to confirm identities at HQ if you've already got past the fish,' Clarke sneered.

Mickey felt herself blushing. She was trying so hard to get everything right.

'We're just waiting for Rupert. Ah, here he is,' Coby said.

Rupert came bustling into the room leading a pack of a dozen rats who were following him in rows of three.

'Operation Shiny Stones

Task Force! Ready and

reporting for duty!

Mission: to

intercept the diamonds

and return them to

their rightful owners,' he called.

All the rats raised their front right paws in a salute then stood to attention.

'Excellent. Clarke and Mickey, are you ready?' Coby asked.

Clarke got to his feet and drawled, 'Operation Scared Dog Team. Agent Clarke and Trial Agent Small Human.'

Clarke turned to Mickey. 'I suppose you'd better follow me.' He darted down the corridor with more speed than Mickey had anticipated, but there was no way she was going to be left behind. She made sure her spy kit was securely fastened then bolted after him.

Clarke spoke to her over his shoulder as he dashed off.

'Remember, I can't speak to you in public unless we're alone or it's very noisy. It pains me to say this but if you do need to speak to me urgently the best thing to do is . . .' Clarke swallowed as if he were swallowing a bitter pill, '. . . pick me up like a pet so you can whisper in my ear. But don't do it unless it's absolutely essential or I'll scratch you.'

Mickey made a note that she would be trying very hard not to do that.

'Follow me at a short distance. Not so far away that you get lost but not close enough that you step on my tail.'

Mickey knew she would not be standing on any tails, but she did have one question.

'You're a cat,' she began.

'Excellent observation skills,' he cut in sarcastically.

'And Rupert's a rat,' Mickey continued, doing her best to ignore his rudeness. 'So it must be quite easy for you two to get around a city. But what about Astrid and Tilda? And what about Bertie? How does he got to and from the headquarters—surely people would notice a giraffe walking down the street?'

'You'd think so, wouldn't you?' the cat replied. 'But the thing about humans is that they don't often look further than the end of their own noses. If they did they might be rather surprised. Anyway, that's enough chat, we have a mission to carry out.'

Chapter
13

The Grand Hotel loomed impressively in front
of them. Mickey was about to ask Clarke how
they were going to get inside without raising
suspicion when he hissed, 'See you in there!'
Then he shot through a gap in the hotel's
railings that was definitely too small for a
human to fit through, even if that human had
studied gymnastics all her life.

Instead, Mickey decided to channel her
inner spy and, despite a quaking feeling, forced
herself to walk towards the main entrance—
trying her very best not to look suspicious.

She went through the revolving doors and
immediately ran into two large security guards
who were blocking the entrance.

'Good evening, miss,' one of them said
formally. 'Do you have your invitation please?'

To her horror, Mickey felt her mind go
blank. She took a deep breath to steady her

thoughts. She had to get this right. She wouldn't be able to convince Clarke that you didn't need to be a grown-up to be a spy if she couldn't even get into the building!

She smiled up at the guard.

'I'm afraid I don't have one, but my uncle left his backpack behind.' She gestured to her spy kit. 'It's very important that he gets it back. Would it be okay if I just ran in quickly to give it to him?'

The guard looked around doubtfully. 'Can you see him from here?''

Mickey pointed to a group gathered in the corridor behind the guards. 'He's over there. His name is . . .' She paused while her brain rattled through the most common men's names . . . 'CHRIS,' she called loudly, while waving wildly.

To Mickey's delight, one of the women in the group nudged a tall man who turned around and waved back, squinting to see who was calling his name.

'That's very sweet, I'm sure he will be pleased,' said the guard. 'But be as quick as you can—this is a very important event and children aren't really allowed in.'

Mickey reckoned that rats, cats, and cobras probably weren't welcome either and wondered if Clarke might be right about how little some grown-ups saw of what was happening around them. She walked towards Chris—but as soon as she heard the guard talking to the next guest she made a quick turn and hid behind a large pillar decorated with fairy lights.

'So you're finally here,' hissed Clarke,

appearing from the other side of the pillar.
'What took you so long?'

Mickey was about to retort crossly about
how quick she'd actually been, given the
circumstances, but decided instead it was time
to focus on the task at hand.

'Where's Winston?' she asked.

'This way.' Clarke turned and led her down
a corridor into the ballroom. There were
pictures of Zadie's new album cover on every
wall and spotlights in all the colours of the
rainbow sending light spiralling around the
room, illuminating a stage area at the front
where a DJ was playing Zadie's best-known
songs. There was a dance floor under a huge
disco ball and several small groups of people
in fancy clothes standing around talking.

Mickey spotted Rupert pressed up against
the wall. He scurried over and swung his way
up to sit on Clarke's head.

'Have a little respect . . . Oof, get off!'
yelped Clarke as Rupert's foot poked him in
the ear.

'Rupert,' whispered Mickey, picking him up

and holding him to her ear so she could talk to him. 'Any sign of the diamond thief?'

'Not yet. We're still scouting all the rooms for clues. We're just doing the ballroom, and I thought I'd come across to wish you jolly good luck on your first assignment.'

'Thanks,' said Mickey. 'I couldn't have been sent anywhere fancier, could I?'

Rupert looked around the glamorous room then pointed to a group of men in smart outfits and frowned.

'Tell me, Mickey. Why do humans always want to look like penguins and never like rats?'

'We-el.' Mickey didn't want to hurt his feelings. 'Maybe they're just easier outfits to find in the shops. The rat look is much rarer.'

'I suppose you're right,' said Rupert, stroking his whiskers. 'Anyway, I must continue searching—good luck!'

Mickey looked around to see that Clarke had moved to the far corner of the room and was in deep conversation with Winston, who was wearing a red bow attached to his collar, which was very much at odds with the woeful expression on his face.

'Hello,' said Mickey, but Winston jumped at the sight of her and shied away.

'There's no need to be scared,' said Clarke. 'You're perfectly safe.'

'That's easy for you to say,' replied Winston. 'The party is only just starting and already I'm trying to look after Zadie plus a *spider* landed on me earlier, somebody knocked a drink over and some of it went on my tail, *and* I happen to know this whole building is full of B-A-T-Hs.'

'Winston,' Clarke interrupted. 'No one here would dare do anything to harm Zadie, or her dog. Not in such a public place.'

'Perhaps we should still monitor the room,' said Mickey, slightly concerned by Clarke's nonchalance.

'Well, why don't you take a walk around, look out for anything suspicious, and I'll stay here with Winston.'

Winston seemed to like this plan. He shuffled himself into the space between

Clarke and a large potted tree decorated with baubles bearing Zadie's signature.

'And you're sure you'll be okay without me?' said Mickey.

'I think we'll manage.' Clarke rolled his eyes.

Mickey stood and scanned the room from left to right and back again, considering her options.

'So you've got a new h-h-human? What happened to Harry?' asked Winston.

'Don't know. Eaten by lions probably,' said Clarke breezily.

'Lions?!' yelped Winston. 'I'm scared of lions!'

For a minute Mickey wondered if Harry really *had* been eaten by lions (and if there were any big cats she herself should be avoiding) as no one from COBRA seemed to know exactly where Harry was. For the first time, she wondered just how risky joining a gang of animal spies might be.

Having analysed the risks of the current situation (they were in a very public place and there were lots of people around, plus Rupert and his field rats) Mickey decided to begin making her way around the crowded room. At one point she thought she'd caught sight of Zadie herself, but lots of other people immediately got in the way and the pop star vanished from view.

Mickey swerved to avoid being hit by a group of particularly enthusiastic dancers and positioned herself by the refreshments table where she could stealthily scan the room and help herself to a strawberry tart or two.

Suddenly there was a

huge
crash

as a
waiter
sent a
tray loaded
with glittery
cupcakes flying.

77

Security closed in immediately, but the commotion unsettled Mickey. Clarke had seemed confident that Winston was fine, but she decided to check up on him.

She returned to their spot, but there was no sign of Clarke or Winston. Mickey looked around frantically and spotted Clarke's tail hanging down from a stone window ledge. Resisting the urge to pull it, Mickey ran over and lifted him down.

Clarke narrowed his eyes and hissed furiously at her. Holding her ground, Mickey held him close to her face and whispered in his ear.

'Where's Winston?'

'Still hiding behind the plant pot of course,' he replied. 'That clumsy waiter dropped a tray and I thought I'd come up here and get a better view of the room.

The window was open so I was just doing a quick check on the grounds.'

Keeping a firm hold on Clarke, Mickey dashed back to check behind the plant pot and, with a growing sense of dread, realized Winston wasn't there either, but the red bow that had been attached to his collar lay there on the ground.

'But I just saw him, right there!' said Clarke. He leapt out of Mickey's arms, landed feet first on the ground, and dropped his jaw in surprise. 'Where's he gone?'

'That's just what I was asking you!' said Mickey, impatiently. 'Do you think someone's taken him?'

Clarke quickly scanned the room, his whiskers twitching while he thought. 'There's no way Winston would have wandered off on his own. Or have removed the bow. Which means he's in trouble. Come on—we have to move quickly!'

Chapter
14

Mickey and Clarke raced out of the ballroom and down the corridor, skidding to a halt outside the next set of doors.

'Dog hairs!' said Clarke, prodding the hairs lying on the ground with his front paw. 'Winston has been here.' Then he turned to Mickey. 'If you wouldn't mind . . .?' he asked.

Mickey, understanding the problem, leaned over and turned the handle of the door.

Clarke stalked inside, and Mickey was close behind. The room was clearly being used as a backstage area for the party—there was a table strewn with paper and pens and a half-eaten plate of food. Under the window, there was a dog basket with 'Winston' embroidered on the front. It was empty. Just then, there was the sound of footsteps coming down the corridor. Mickey froze and listened as they grew louder and then stopped right outside the door.

'Quick, under the table!' hissed Clarke, diving for cover. Mickey scrambled to join him but had further to go to get to the ground so was a little slower. Just as she pulled her feet in the door swung open.

From their hiding place, they watched as two sets of shoes came into the room: one, a pair of high, glittery silver heels peeping from under a long and floaty purple dress; the other, a pair of heavy-duty, thick-soled black boots beneath dark trousers.

'Thanks for the hot lemon. I think that's really done the trick for my vocal cords,' said a female voice.

Zadie! thought Mickey excitedly.

'Excellent, ma'am. It's an old family recipe. Now, we must get you to the stage. There's five minutes until your performance.'

'Nearly ready! Just changing these earrings.' There was a jangling sound that Mickey knew was Zadie adding her signature chandelier earrings to her look. 'Has anyone seen Winston? I thought he had been brought here to sleep in his basket, but it's empty.'

'I'll be sure to check, but we really must get to the stage.'

'Yeah, I know. I wish I didn't always get so nervous.' Zadie sighed loudly. 'Winston always calms me down.' Then both pairs of shoes turned and left the room.

As soon as the door closed, Mickey let out a deep breath that she hadn't realized she'd been holding.

'Maybe Winston *was* taken back here, like Zadie said. There might be a clue about where he is now!' Mickey whispered.

Clarke was one step ahead of her as he walked round the basket swishing his tail.

'There's nothing of interest here,' he reported.

Mickey moved over to take a closer look. She lifted the padded cushion from Winston's basket and felt all around the edges, but there was nothing there. As Clarke was peering over to double-check, they both heard a noise outside the window. It sounded like a faint whine followed by a sharp bark, which was quickly muffled . . .

Mickey jumped up and pulled at the window, but it was jammed shut.

'Try wiggling it,' Clarke said urgently.

Mickey tried and it wobbled slightly then reluctantly slid open a few inches. She knew she would never fit through, but Clarke might . . . They looked at one another and a moment of understanding passed between them. Clarke leapt up on to the windowsill.

'Follow that noise!' cried Mickey.

Clarke wasted no time and sprang out into the evening air, while Mickey desperately continued trying to yank the window open further, but it wouldn't budge. She decided the best thing she could do was to continue searching the hotel for clues and hope Clarke could track down Winston.

Barrelling out of the room, Mickey carried out a detailed sweep of the ground floor of the building, looking for any signs of Winston. She checked corridors and the lounge area. As she hurried past the breakfast room, she heard muffled sounds coming from one of the nearby guest bedrooms. She glanced at her watch. It was nearly 7 p.m.—the time of the diamond handover.

As Mickey approached, the door swung open a crack and a cream-coloured cat slunk out. Mickey looked more closely. The cat was startling, with one blue eye and one green eye. Where had Mickey seen that cat before?

'Ruby?' she asked. This was the footballer's cat—the one who had claimed not to know anything about the missing diamonds! What was she doing here?

At the sight of Mickey, the cat shot down the corridor and out of sight. Mickey considered following, but there were so many

nooks and crannies in this hotel, Ruby could be anywhere by now.

Mickey hoped beyond hope that Clarke had managed to locate Winston and, not for the first time, wondered if there *was* a link between Winston's fears and the diamond thefts.

She pulled out her notebook to write down the number of the room Ruby had come out of—**Room 103**—then put the book safely away, tiptoed up to the door, and placed her ear against it.

'I have the diamonds,' came a low, rather muffled voice from inside the room.

With a jolt, Mickey remembered the message:

BRING ME THE DIAMONDS
THE GRAND HOTEL
ASK FOR MIA
7 PM 14TH JUNE

Mickey must have stumbled across 'Mia'! As she leaned even closer to the door, her spy kit swung round, making a gentle thud against the door, and she froze, hoping they hadn't heard her.

To her horror, she heard Mia getting to her feet and then heavy footsteps getting louder as they moved towards the hotel room's door. If Mickey was caught now, she could blow the whole operation! Rupert might already be in there, ready to retrieve the diamonds, and she couldn't risk messing things up. She turned on her heels and fled, not stopping until she was safely out of the hotel.

Her brain quickly went into overdrive. If she had just stumbled across the diamond handover, that meant Mia now had the diamonds. And if Ruby had just left the very same room, then not only had Ruby lied about not knowing what had happened to the diamonds—but it looked like she was the one who had taken them!

Mickey waited for the satisfying feeling of solving a puzzle, but it didn't come. And then she realized that Winston was still missing, possibly dognapped, and the diamond thief wasn't a person at all, but quite possibly a cat!

She had a feeling that neither of these pieces of information was going to go down terribly well at COBRA HQ.

Chapter 15

Mickey was right. It went down very badly. She'd run all the way back to **COBRA** HQ, which, as someone who didn't much like running around during games, had made her vow to work on her stamina and fitness. With her heart still hammering in her chest, Mickey told the story to the High Committee—minus Clarke, who hadn't made it back yet, and Rupert, who was still on patrol with the rats.

'Just to be clear,' hissed Coby in a dangerous voice, 'you're saying that you lost Winston, you think he's been dognapped, and that a noble *animal,* rather than a human, is responsible for taking the diamonds?'

There was an audible gasp from Astrid and a slower one from Tilda, which echoed around the room.

'Yes.' Mickey stood her ground. 'Ruby, the

footballer's cat, must have taken them. And I think there's a connection to Winston's disappearance. I just haven't figured out what it is yet.'

'I don't think Ruby would do that. She's very trustworthy,' said Astrid. 'We've worked with her for years.'

'What wouldn't Ruby do?' asked Clarke as he stalked into the room.

'That can wait,' hissed Coby, turning to him. 'Did you lose Winston?'

Clarke paused and caught Mickey's gaze. She was holding her breath, desperately hoping he had found Winston.

'Unfortunately so,' confessed Clarke. 'There was a commotion in the ballroom and while I was investigating someone must have swooped in and taken him. All we could find was the bow he'd been wearing for the party. I tried searching for him but, unfortunately, it was in vain—and since I couldn't find Mickey anywhere after that I came back to report to HQ.'

'I can't believe an agent of your standing

would make such a terrible mistake,' said Coby.

'Well, since you insisted I take the small human along for the mission, it is hardly surprising that things didn't go entirely to plan,' Clarke said, as haughtily as ever. 'I only have one pair of eyes, but I had *two* creatures to babysit: the dog and the girl.'

'We need to find Winston, and quickly,' said Coby, rolling his eyes. 'I don't want to give the domestic animals further reason to be distrustful of our organization, and it appears that Winston was right to be worried.'

'I briefed Rupert back at the hotel and asked him and the others to switch their focus to finding Winston. It's possible they are on their way back with the dog right now,' said Clarke, looking pleased with himself.

'And I wonder if Rupert can explain why he missed the diamond drop while our small human claims to have witnessed it,' Coby hissed.

Clarke scoffed. 'The rats were looking for a suspicious *person*. Did I hear Mickey

saying Ruby was somehow involved? She is
an impeccable pet, and any implication she
is involved is quite simply a mistake. And we
shouldn't take Mickey's word for it. After all,
Winston went missing on *her* watch.'

Mickey's cheeks flared red.

'I didn't make a mistake. It was definitely
Ruby! And Clarke was the one who lost
Winston, not me!' she said crossly.

'Well, *you* are the one accusing an innocent
cat of a crime they almost certainly did not
commit!' snapped Clarke. 'I *knew* a *human*
cub would make a terrible spy.'

Mickey looked over to Astrid. Surely she
would be on her side?

'It is a little hard to believe,' Astrid said.
And Mickey felt her hopes dim.

'Indeed,' agreed Coby. 'None of our
intelligence flagged up that Ruby could be a
suspect. She is a feline of excellent standing
and has worked closely with COBRA on
several missions over the years.'

Mickey may not have worked with COBRA
over several years—this was her very first

mission—but she knew what she'd seen, and it was so frustrating that she couldn't make them believe her! This was just like when adults made up their minds and wouldn't listen to her just because they were older.

'Tilda, has there been anything in the files that suggests that Ruby could have been compromised?' Mickey asked desperately.

Tilda paused and leafed through a big file that had been sitting under her desk. Mickey let herself hope Tilda would find something.

While they were waiting, Mickey turned to the other animals pleadingly. 'Winston going missing, the diamonds, Mia, Ruby . . . they are all connected, I'm sure of it. Winston was scared of something. What if he knew someone was out to get him? What if he knew something about the diamond thefts, or . . . or . . . that the diamond thief was Ruby and she was threatening Winston to keep quiet?'

Tilda slowly looked up from her papers. 'Ruby's file is clean.'

'Right,' said Coby, snapping her head up straight. 'This has been a terrible evening all around. Mickey, your theories are hot air. You have no proof, and we have a missing dog to find—a dog that you and Clarke were tasked with protecting. We have also failed in our mission to intercept the diamonds, causing terrible damage to our reputation. We need to get this situation under control quickly, and I think we'd find that easier without a newbie hanging around. Astrid, would you please show Mickey out?'

'What?' cried Mickey. This couldn't be happening. 'But what about Winston? What if he's behind a locked door and you can't work the handles?'

This was the wrong thing to say. Coby raised her head to its highest height and

hissed furiously.

93

'Do not underestimate the power of **COBRA**. We will return to our usual way of working in order to find Winston and the diamonds.'

Defeated, Mickey slung her spy kit on her back and reluctantly followed Astrid to the exit.

'I'm so sorry it's ended this way,' said Astrid, patting Mickey's hand with one of her spindly arms.

Mickey quite agreed—nothing had gone the way she had hoped. Perhaps **COBRA** had been right and kids couldn't be spies after all.

Chapter
16

Mickey couldn't think of a time when she'd felt as bad as this. All the happy hopeful feelings she'd had when she'd been accepted by **COBRA** had gone, leaving her with a horrible emptiness. But even worse was knowing Winston was still missing and she wasn't allowed to be part of the mission to get him back.

She stomped all the way back to her block of flats and snuck back into her room, where she threw herself down on her bed and stared firmly at the wall—no codes, no animals, no mission. Eventually her eyes felt heavy, and she fell asleep.

Mickey woke up the next morning to the same horrible feeling. As she got dressed, the picture of Hildegarde she had stuck to her mirror caught her eye. Mickey tried not to look at it, but it kept drawing her gaze. With a gloomy sigh she sat herself up and looked at the quotation on it:

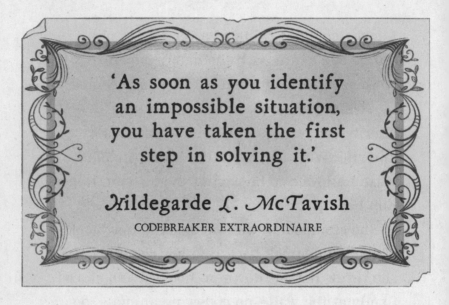

'As soon as you identify an impossible situation, you have taken the first step in solving it.'

Hildegarde L. McTavish

CODEBREAKER EXTRAORDINAIRE

COBRA was definitely an impossible situation.

Mickey lay on her back, with her head hanging over the end of her bed—an unusual angle that helped her think more clearly.

A good codebreaker is one who solves problems all the way to the end. And **COBRA** might think this was the end, but Mickey certainly did not. Hildegarde L. McTavish wouldn't take no for an answer, and neither would Mickey R. Thompson, who realized that in the absence of any clues about Winston's whereabouts the only thing she could do was work with what she had. And she had one piece of information that **COBRA** did not—she knew what she'd seen that night at the hotel. **COBRA** might not be interested in pursuing Ruby, but maybe she could investigate on her own?

There were just three things she needed:

1. RUBY'S ADDRESS.
2. DIRECTIONS TO THAT ADDRESS.
3. A PLAN—NEED TO THINK OF THIS QUICKLY!

Mickey sat herself the right way up then went to her desk and took out her notebook. She forced herself to think back through recent events. Coby had mentioned that the famous footballer Alexi Holt lived on one of the most expensive streets in the country, but she couldn't remember the name of it. She took another deep breath and let her mind wander. Years ago she had read that the best way to remember information was to picture it. So if you had a new teacher called Mrs Baker, you might picture her holding a cake or a loaf of bread. Mickey had tried to deploy this tactic whenever bits of information came up, as you never knew when they would come in useful. Suddenly her mind filled with the image of a majestic brown bird with a white head and a big yellow beak. 'An eagle,' Mickey muttered. That was it! The address was Eagle Gardens. Mickey felt a shiver of excitement. The mission wasn't over yet.

It took Mickey a good twenty minutes to walk to Eagle Gardens from the nearest bus stop. The houses stretching before her were huge, white buildings surrounded by large fences that gleamed in the sun.

There weren't many signs of animal activity, but Mickey kept her eyes peeled. She heard a scuffling sound and whipped round to see a cat run out of a gate and under a nearby car. Mickey noticed the eyes straight away—it was Ruby.

It was time to follow a suspect without being noticed. Mickey swiftly altered her route and followed the cat from car to car, until they came to an alley behind a small cafe, which was full of cardboard boxes and smelt quite strongly of fish. Ruby paused to take in the delicious scent, and Mickey leapt behind an oil drum, pulling her T-shirt over her nose to try to cover the smell.

From her hiding place, Mickey peered over the top of the drum and saw Ruby meeting up with two other animals—Thor and Max, the dogs mentioned in the briefing at **COBRA**!

Mickey's brain was whirring—why were these animals slinking around, meeting up in secret? There was something going on, she was sure of it. Mickey pulled her phone out of her pocket to take a picture.

She took time to carefully frame the photo, making sure all three animals were in shot, and then . . .

SNAP!!!

The phone's camera made a sharp clicking sound. Oh. She thought she'd put it on silent mode—what an amateur! Making a mental note to check this *every time,* Mickey lifted her gaze from the camera to see Ruby and the two dogs staring straight at her.

Chapter
17

'Take your time,' she told herself. 'They don't know who you are.' Thinking quickly, she reached over to Max the sheepdog as if to pat him.

'Oh, hello there—what a good dog!' she said, hoping she could pass herself off as someone who just really liked dogs. 'Aren't you lovely?' The dog rolled over and smiled happily, and Mickey honestly thought she might be about to get away with it.

But then Ruby, who had been watching her with narrowed eyes, suddenly let out a loud hiss and Mickey knew she must have recognized her from the hotel. It was time to make a quick getaway.

'Good dog,' she repeated to Max as she got to her feet. But when she turned around to leave, Thor—the Leonberger dog—was blocking her way. He was massive, the biggest dog Mickey had ever seen, and although he was very fluffy he was baring his teeth and holding his ears and tail high as if ready to spring for an attack.

He gave a warning bark, and Max and Ruby sprang to join him so that Mickey was completely surrounded.

Backed into a corner, there was only one thing she could think of to do. Very carefully, so as not to spook the animals with a sudden movement, she moved her hand up towards her face and carefully tapped her head three times to make the **COBRA** greeting sign.

Ruby blinked three times in response. 'How do you know about **COBRA**?' she asked.

'I'm in **COBRA**!' Mickey replied. 'Or, I was. I might be. It's all a bit confusing. I'm Mickey, the new human recruit?' she tried to explain.

'Probably needed someone with opposable thumbs,' said Thor, blinking his eyes three times.

'I'm blinking, too, but you probably can't see under all my hair! Why didn't you say earlier?' cried Max the sheepdog, turning in a circle. 'This is excellent timing! Thor, aren't you pleased you didn't try to eat someone from COBRA?'

'I wasn't *actually* going to eat her,' said Thor huffily. However, he did seem keen to make amends and, as there were no seats in the alley, he bent down to offer Mickey his back as a rest. She politely declined, and instead sat down on the ground amongst the gang of three.

'You know about COBRA?' she checked.

'Who doesn't? Well, apart from humans—no offence,' said Thor.

'And you're all animals whose humans have had diamonds stolen?' Mickey continued.

All three nodded slowly.

'And I suspect you know more than you've been admitting to COBRA?'

They looked guiltily at the ground.

'Why haven't you been talking to them?' asked Mickey.

'Because we were told not to,' said Max quietly. 'They said if we breathed a word to any animals from COBRA then our owners

would be in Huge Danger.'

'But I'm a human, not an animal,' said
Mickey. 'Were you warned about speaking to
humans?'

'No!' cried Max.

Thor looked like a light bulb had just gone
off above his head, 'Aha—a loophole. I think
we can tell her, Ruby!'

'I suppose we could use the help,' said
Ruby. 'Though it is quite a long story.'

Chapter

18

'I'm listening,' said Mickey, taking her notebook out of her spy kit to make notes.

'We're being blackmailed by a thief called Mia,' Ruby began. 'Max's owner had her diamonds stolen first. And when the same thing happened to Thor's owner, all the pets started to worry. If a dog like Thor couldn't protect his house, what chance did the hamsters and guinea pigs have?'

'Of course,' said Mickey, scribbling this down in her notebook.

'And then it happened to me,' Ruby went on. 'I was out patrolling my area one evening when somebody scooped me up from nowhere and everything went dark. I think they put me in a pillowcase, but I couldn't feel the ground underneath me and it was very strange. Then a human voice said: "We want Alexi's diamond necklace. You need to get it and bring it to us. We'll let you know when. And we know all about COBRA. Don't breathe a word to them or any of the other" . . .' Ruby paused for the next word '. . . "*mangy* pets, or you won't see your Alexi ever again. We'll tell you when to bring the diamonds to us. Don't be late."'

'So this was Mia? Did you see what she looked like?' asked Mickey.

'Not really, but she was a human,' explained Ruby. 'She was human-shaped and had blonde hair. And she was wearing gloves.'

'Maybe to avoid leaving fingerprints!' said Mickey.

'But then I was in the pillowcase and couldn't see anything,' said Ruby. 'She said I had to do it because only a pet is trusted to go all around a house—even in rooms with valuables—and it wouldn't look suspicious. Thor, Max, and I didn't know what to do because we couldn't talk to COBRA about it. And we couldn't risk harm coming to our owners. We love them, and we were trying to protect them!'

'Have any other pets been approached to steal jewels?' Mickey asked.

'Mia tried to get Winston to steal from Zadie, but he wouldn't do it. We were all afraid of what might happen next, but Winston couldn't bear to do it. She wanted him to steal Zadie's most precious possession: her ring, which is a family heirloom. She doesn't even wear it in public very often because it is so special to her. He's so brave.'

'He is,' said Mickey, remembering the trembling spaniel. 'But he's gone missing—

the harm came to him, not his owner. We need to get him back!'

'Winston is missing?' asked Thor. 'I saw him last week, and he told me he'd tried to ask **COBRA** for help but couldn't tell them the whole story because there was a human in the HQ.'

Mickey suddenly realized why Winston had been so reluctant to come near her—he must have thought she was working with the diamond thief!'

'It happened last night,' said Mickey gently. 'I don't want any harm to come to him. We need to find Winston! No harm has come to Zadie yet, but things could change and he might have been dognapped so they can ask for a ransom!'

'Do you think you can help get him back?' asked Ruby quickly.

'I will do my very best,' Mickey replied, reaching out her hand to reassure Ruby, whose whiskers were drooping. 'Coby will know what to do.'

'But Mia said we weren't to tell any of the

animals at **COBRA**.'

'But you haven't,' pointed out Mickey. 'I'll tell them. And I'm a human.'

Mickey could feel her heart beating quickly as her brain clicked the pieces into place. She'd got it wrong when she thought Ruby was behind the diamond thefts—but not completely wrong, as Mia had been forcing the animals to do her bidding. The missing dog and the missing diamonds were linked— and by a person who knew all about **COBRA** and someone who might be about to issue a ransom for Winston's safe return.

Things were getting dangerous. She needed to warn **COBRA** and she *really* hoped they would believe her.

'Ruby, when you handed over the diamonds to the thief at the hotel last night, did you see what she looked like?'

'Not really. She had a lot of blonde wavy hair,' replied Ruby. 'But now I know Winston's missing, I think I *heard* something useful.' She looked at Mickey, her big eyes filling with sadness. 'There was a sort of muffled scratching sound from the room! I thought maybe there was another animal involved—but WHAT IF IT WAS WINSTON AND HE WAS TRAPPED?'

With a jolt, Mickey realized the cat may have hit on something. It could have been Winston. When she and Clarke had heard a bark from outside, that could have been Mia moving Winston from the ballroom to **Room 103**. It would explain why Clarke found no trace of Winston when he went through the window to investigate.

There was no time to lose. They had to get to **COBRA** HQ immediately.

Chapter

19

Mickey and Ruby stood in the entrance of
COBRA HQ, waiting patiently for the goldfish
to do the head-tapping trick, but instead
the goldfish just swam round and round in
circles, ignoring them.

'You're not an official **COBRA** member, so
you don't have special privileges to bring in
guests,' said Clarke, slinking in behind them.
'Is that . . . Ruby?'

'Hello, Clarke,' said Ruby. 'Can you
sign us in quickly please? There's
something important we need to explain to

the committee.'

Clarke put on his best manners, which Mickey had never seen him use before. 'Certainly.' He nodded to the goldfish. 'Ruby is with me, and I suppose the small human is too.'

The fish tapped its tank, the wall swung back, and Mickey and the two cats stepped through.

'I hope you're not always this unfriendly to new recruits, Clarke,' said Ruby, as she trotted down the corridor.

'Oh *really,*' said Clarke's haughty voice. 'Well the last time *this one* was here she was accusing you of a crime! Of course I told her she must be mistaken.'

'She wasn't really,' explained Ruby. 'Is everyone here?'

Clarke nodded and held open the door while Ruby swanned past and into the meeting room. Mickey darted in behind her and Clarke grimaced but kept holding the door before letting it close once she was safely through.

Coby, Rupert, Astrid, and Tilda were sitting around the table, which was covered in pictures of Winston. They all looked up as Mickey and the two cats approached.

'Mickey . . .' Coby said. 'And Ruby . . . What a surprise to see you both . . . and together?'

Mickey looked at Ruby and whispered, 'I'll explain,' before turning to fill in Coby on everything she had learned from Ruby, Max, and Thor.

'Ruby was involved in the diamond drop, but it wasn't her fault,' Mickey began. 'Mia has been blackmailing the animals to steal from their owners—and threatening them if they refuse to do as she says. Winston refused to steal from Zadie, so we think Mia's dognapped him and will issue a ransom—probably for the ring he wouldn't steal—any minute now. But there's another problem because Mia specifically told them not to speak to any animals from COBRA, which means she knows about your secret organization.'

'What?!' said Coby, flaring her hooded neck. 'Did you tell someone about us?'

'It couldn't have been Mickey,' said Astrid quickly. 'Mia was already causing trouble before she found us.'

'Harry then!' hissed Coby. 'He's the only other person who knows about us, he must be working with Mia! Unreliable *and* a traitor! There is no time to lose. I hereby combine our two previous missions Operation Shiny Stones and Operation Scared Dog into one which shall henceforth be known as Operation Shiny Dog. Mickey, you showed great initiative in tracking down Ruby and bringing her back to us.'

'Bravo . . . Mickey,' said Tilda, her mouth stretching very slowly into a grin, as Astrid flashed her a thumbs up with her foot.

'I suppose Mickey did do a good job,' said Clarke reluctantly.

Was that a compliment? Mickey whipped her head round to be sure she'd heard him correctly.

'Right,' said Coby. 'We have more

information now, but we also have two pesky humans to track down and we need to move quickly. Clarke—I need you to check with all the pets and our networks to see if any other animals have been blackmailed. Tilda—you and I will go through the notes we have so far and speak to all the animals who were blackmailed by Mia. I want Winston found and Mia and Harry stopped. Mickey and Astrid—go and investigate **Room 103** at the hotel, to see if you can find any clues there.' Coby was still hissing out orders. 'Rupert—I want the field rats to surround Zadie's house and keep watch for a ransom note. It is crucial we get the information contained in it as quickly as possible. Ideally we will return Winston before a demand is issued, but it's best to be prepared.' Coby paused. 'I'm sure I don't need to remind you all that the future of **COBRA** rests on the success of this mission. Operation Shiny Dog needs to bring Winston back safely, stop the diamond thieves, and restore trust in **COBRA** among the wider animal community. Let's get to work.'

REPORT

Briefing report on Mia

Notes taken by Tilda upon
interview of witness: Ruby

Name: Mia

Age: ?

Height:
Taller than a cat,
shorter than a giraffe

Description:
Wavy blonde hair, wears
gloves

Chapter
20

Mickey was thrilled to be part of the gang again, and she and Astrid dashed outside, eager to find clues to bring Winston home, but they quickly ran into their first problem. **The Grand Hotel** was too far for Astrid to walk to (even if she could stay hidden from humans by stealth) and she was too long to fit in the backpack.

'My arms and legs will stick out!' she explained. 'And I need to be able to see what's going on.'

Mickey thought hard. Astrid was a slightly difficult shape to hide, and her long limbs meant she also couldn't just perch in a pocket like Rupert could. Unless . . .

'I know!' Mickey cried. 'You can be a novelty backpack!'

'I beg your pardon?' asked Astrid.

'It's perfect!' said Mickey, seeing the plan

unfold in front of her. She slung her spy kit on and turned to show Astrid how the straps fitted over her shoulder.

'See? No one would ever guess, and you'll be able to see everything. *And* you won't have to do any walking.' Having explained, Mickey took off her backpack.

'That is an excellent plan,' Astrid relented, hopping on.

Holding her spy kit in her left hand, Mickey made her way back over to **The Grand Hotel** with Astrid on her back.

The building was quieter in the daytime.
There were no security guards on duty,
so Mickey sauntered past, smiling at the
receptionists and doing her best to look like
a child on holiday who didn't have a care in
the world and definitely didn't have a spider
monkey on her back.

She retraced her steps from the previous
night and walked Astrid over to **Room 103**.

'How are we going to get in?' whispered
Astrid.

That, Mickey thought, was a very good
question. But first she had to check there
wasn't anybody in the room. It was no good
getting through the door only to be chased out
by an angry holidaymaker.

Mickey took a deep breath, walked up to
the door, and tapped on it firmly.

Nothing happened.

She waited for a minute then tried again.

This time the door swung open to reveal a

man in the middle of tying a scarf around his neck, a minty smell of toothpaste in the air.

Mickey felt Astrid's grip tighten around her neck as the monkey slid further down her back.

'Yes?' the man asked briskly.

'Sorry!' Mickey said. 'I thought this was my room!'

'Clearly not,' the man replied, and then he closed the door before she had a chance to ask anything else.

Astrid waited a moment, then tugged on Mickey's ear.

'Do you know what I just noticed?' she whispered.

Mickey's brain had also been whirring. 'I know. The scarf and the toothpaste smell mean he's probably getting ready to go out. We'll be able to get in soon!'

'That's not the only thing,' Astrid whispered. 'That's not just any man—that's Harry!'

Chapter 21

'Harry?' gasped Mickey. 'The one who's been missing for months? The one Coby thinks told Mia about **COBRA**?'

'The very same Harry,' replied Astrid.

Before they had a chance to discuss further, the door to **Room 103** opened again and Harry headed off down the hall without even giving Mickey a second glance, or noticing the spider monkey on her back.

'All clear,' said Astrid.

'We need to check the room quickly. We don't know how long he'll be,' said Mickey. 'And Mia could also turn up at any time.'

'How do we get in?' asked Astrid.

Mickey had been pondering this.

'Harry used a key to lock the room. The hotel must keep spares somewhere. They're probably behind the reception desk.'

'I'll go and look,' said Astrid. 'Spider

monkeys are very stealthy. I'll be right back.'

'Okay, but you mustn't be seen!' Mickey
urged.

'I know,' the spider monkey reassured her.
'I have a plan.'

She climbed up the curtain then leapt from
curtain rail to picture frame to light fitting so
she didn't even touch the floor. And no sooner
had she gone than she was back, swinging
happily, her tail neatly tucked around a spare
key for **Room 103**. Mickey unlocked the door,
and she and Astrid scrambled in.

Mickey checked the drawers, the bedside
table, and the mattress—while Astrid hopped
along the top of the wardrobe and dived
under the bed.

'Nothing here,' Astrid reported. 'Shall we
try the bathroom?'

Mickey turned the handle, and they both
scanned the room.

Astrid ran straight to the bath mat and
held up a few fine blonde hairs.

'Mia's?' asked Mickey.

'Maybe this one,' said Astrid, separating a

wavy hair from the others. 'But these are dog hairs.' She held up three short golden hairs.

'So Winston *was* here?' Mickey said.

'I can't believe Harry is involved with all this. That dastardly human!' cried Astrid.

Mickey stared around the bathroom again. If Winston had been trapped here, would he have had time to leave a message somewhere? She looked in the cupboard under the sink and pulled out a blonde wig.

'Look, Astrid!' She held it up. 'Isn't this the hairstyle Ruby described?'

'Yes!' cried the monkey. Then her face fell. 'Does that mean Mia might have changed her hair?'

Mickey was quickly scanning the bathroom as she suddenly realized there was one thing she and Astrid had completely overlooked. There was one toothbrush sitting next to the sink and one bath towel hanging over the rail. Mickey ran into the main bedroom and saw a pair of pyjamas tucked neatly under one of the pillows and one small suitcase sitting in the corner. She ran back into the bathroom.

'Astrid! It looks like there's only one person staying in this room. If we found the wig, do you think we might be looking for one person, not two? I think "Mia" is Harry in disguise and the wig was designed to throw us off the scent!'

Astrid's jaw dropped. 'But. . . but the message said "ask for Mia" and Ruby described her. Unless that's what Harry *wanted us to think*!'

'He's clever. Annoying, but clever,' said Mickey.

'That's the problem with Harry,' said Astrid. 'He's very, very clever. If he's the one behind the diamond thefts and Winston's disappearance, Coby is going to be furious. Harry has betrayed us all.'

Harry sounded like a nasty piece of work—Mickey couldn't bear the thought of Winston feeling alone and scared. There must be something in this room that would help to solve this puzzle. She remembered Hildegarde's insistence on the need to look at a problem *differently* in order to solve it.

Mickey climbed into the bath and hung
carefully over the side. Astrid looked bemused
but then hopped in and lowered herself down
into the same position

'What are we doing?' she asked, not
unreasonably.

'Looking,' Mickey replied.

Things might have been strange and
growing stranger by the second, but she
still had her tried-and-trusted techniques.
She gazed around the upside-down room

and moved her eyes up and down and criss-crossed, looking for clues. Then her eyes flicked to the underside of the windowsill. There was something underneath. She put herself the right way up and dashed over to look, with Astrid following. There, written in wobbly red writing—maybe written by a scared dog wielding a pen in his paws—were the words:

RS STORAGE

'What's a RS STORAGE?' asked Astrid. 'Is that a human thing?'

Mickey had seen something similar on a poster on the bus . . . It was a storage company that had an unusual name. She just needed to remember it . . .

'Red Squirrel Storage!' she cried. 'Maybe he heard where they're taking him . . . He could still be there. We need to go

right now!'

Chapter

22

'We need to tell Coby!' said Astrid as they slipped out of the room .

'But what if they're about to move Winston?' Mickey asked, once they were safely outside, dropping the key next to the reception desk on their way past. 'We may not have much time.'

'We could send Coby a B-Mail,' said Astrid. 'Then she could meet us there?'

'B-Mail?' said Mickey.

'Short for Bird-Mail. You ask a passing bird to fly it to the HQ. They're meant to go straight there, but some are more reliable than others. Owls will only do it at night; seagulls get easily distracted by food. Robins are the best.'

Mickey looked around frantically for a robin. She couldn't see one but did spot a blackbird hopping about outside the hotel.

Mickey approached carefully and tapped her head three times. The bird covered its eyes slowly three times with its wings. Astrid swung round to speak to it.

'We have an URGENT message for **COBRA** HQ,' she said. 'Tell them to meet Astrid and Mickey at Red Squirrel Storage straight away. Please fly as fast as you can.'

The bird chirruped, then flapped its wings and took off—Mickey hoped it would get there quickly.

She looked up the address for Red Squirrel Storage on her phone and, with Astrid secure on her back again, leapt on to a bus. It took forever because they kept running into red lights, and Mickey drummed her fingers on the windowsill impatiently, hoping against hope that Winston would be okay when they got to him.

Finally, they reached their stop. Red Squirrel Storage occupied all the old units on an abandoned industrial estate. Two bored-looking employees with clipboards monitored it from a small hut in the centre of the estate. Mickey ducked behind a large tree on the edge of the estate to take stock of the situation. But as she stepped round, she came face-to-face with Bertie the giraffe. Instead of his usual bow tie, he was wearing a baseball cap and a white label that said '2024'. Bertie was opening his mouth to scream when Clarke swung down from the tree, clamped one paw over the giraffe's mouth, and said, 'It's okay. It's Mickey, remember? She's one of us.'

Chapter 23

Clarke removed his paw from the giraffe's mouth, and Bertie took three big gulps of air, before bending down so his eyes were level with Mickey's.

'Sorry about that,' the giraffe whispered.

'Not a problem,' Mickey replied. Then she turned to Clarke. 'How did you beat us here?'

'Giraffes can run at thirty-one miles per hour,' said Clarke.

'Thirty-seven, if I sprint,' panted Bertie.

'And he doesn't have to stop for red lights,' Clarke added. 'Though we did have to dress him up as a novelty marathon runner—no one ever thinks he's a real giraffe.'

'Oh look, here come the others!' cried Astrid.

Mickey turned to see Coby and Rupert approaching, accompanied by a rather horrible smell.

'Ugh,' said Clarke. 'They took the sewer route. It's quick, but it makes you stink.'

'Apologies,' said Rupert, hopping down from the end of Coby's body.

'Where's Tilda?' asked Coby.

Clarke reached up into the tree and pulled.

Tilda tumbled into view and was neatly caught by Bertie.

'Hello, everyone,' she said. 'I . . . felt a bit sleepy after the long journey . . . Thought I'd have a nap.'

'What's this about Harry coming back?' Coby demanded, her eyes blazing with fury.

'Ah,' said Astrid. 'The good news is we don't think we're after two people—Mia and Harry. The bad news is we think Harry's behind both thefts—dog and diamonds—and was posing as "Mia" to throw us off the scent.'

'WHAT?' Coby spat.

'If I may be so bold . . .' interrupted Tilda, and everyone turned to look at her. 'Winston may be in imminent danger, so we should get him back safely and then worry about Harry.'

'A fair point,' said Rupert. 'Look, here comes a field-rats patrol.'

A dozen damp-looking rats came dashing up, and the strange smell that had arrived with Coby and Rupert got stronger.

'Ugh, they took the sewers too!' said Astrid, wrapping her tail over her nose.

The lead rat ran up to Rupert and saluted.

'Anything to report?' Rupert asked.

'We've spoken to all the wild creatures we can find around this building,' the leader of the rats replied.

'And?' Coby interrupted.

'They said there's been something strange happening with a storage unit at the very back—number 27. A human came by late at night with a large package under their arm that seemed to be moving . . .'

'What are we waiting for? Let's go!' Coby ordered.

The field rats led the way to Unit 27, taking care to go the long way around through the trees, rather than go past the hut with human staff inside.

Clarke bounded ahead and got there first. Mickey was second and saw that Unit 27 was a metal shed with a tightly fitted door with a number panel on it. As the others approached, Clarke turned and nodded towards the door. 'Bad luck. It's a keypad-entry system, and we don't know the code.'

'I can try,' Mickey volunteered, stepping forward. But Coby hissed and wrapped her tail around her wrist to hold her back.

'Wait. We need to check if this is the right unit first.'

'But how?' said Tilda. 'There are no windows.'

'I'll shout—HELLO, IS ANYONE IN THERE?' cried Astrid.

There was no reply.

'No,' said Coby. 'Bertie, can you check the roof? Maybe there's a chimney or an air vent we could use?'

'Happy to,' said the giraffe, stretching himself up to his full height and putting his head all the way up to take a good look around. 'No entry points here,' he called

down. 'Unless . . . unless you can get a spider.
There's a very small crack in one corner.'

Astrid sprang back to the trees and
returned carrying a spider carefully on
her hand.

Coby tapped her head three times with her tail. Mickey couldn't see the spider respond as it was so small, but it seemed to pass since Coby continued. 'We need to know what's inside this container. Can you tell us?' Then Astrid passed the spider to Bertie.

Mickey watched as it scuttled up Bertie's neck then disappeared from sight.

'It's going through the gap,' Bertie called down. Everyone held their breath and hoped the spider would return with good news. A minute later, Bertie called, 'It's back. It says no humans but there's a large cage covered with a cloth and it can hear muffled barks.'

'Excellent work,' said Coby. 'This must be Winston. Mickey, can you do anything with this keypad? If you can't, we might need to get Astrid to contact a larger animal to help us rip the door off.'

'Let me try.' Mickey dashed forward and carefully typed **1234** into the keypad.

'Surely people don't use that as a

security code,' scoffed Clarke.

'You'd be surprised,' murmured Mickey. Unfortunately, today Clarke was right. The door remained stubbornly closed.

'I need more information,' she said, her face scrunched up in concentration. 'Does anyone know the date of Harry's birthday?'

The other animals shook their heads, apart from Astrid who sighed.

'Do none of you pay attention? It's *always* me who remembers birthdays and has to organize the cake and the card—Harry's is the sixth of November.'

Mickey tried **0611** in the keypad, but nothing happened. You weren't really supposed to use your birthday as a security code, but lots of people did. She tried it the other way around—**1106**—but still nothing. Then, in desperation, she tried it backwards. She was running out of ideas. She tried **1160**, crossing her fingers it would work, but it seemed as though luck was against her. Then, just as her heart was sinking, there was a small click and a green light appeared. The door swung open.

Chapter
24

'It's open!' cried Astrid, springing forward. 'Wait,' ordered Coby. 'This could still be a trap. I want everyone to withdraw to safety except for myself, Clarke, the field rats, . . . and Mickey,' she added, looking at Mickey's thumbs.

'Fine,' said Clarke. 'As long as you think Mickey can handle the danger.'

Oddly, Mickey was sure she *could* handle it. Perhaps she was worthy of being a spy after all.

Tilda, Bertie, Astrid, and Rupert retreated to a safe distance and then Coby led the way into the container, accompanied by two of the field rats.

Mickey could see the blanket over the cage as the spider had described. Coby slithered straight up to it, bit on to a corner, then slid back to reveal Winston lying miserably on the floor, staring mournfully at the wall.

'Winston!' one of the field rats called out, running up to him.

'No, no, no, I don't want any SEWER RATS!' cried Winston, shaking like a jelly and burying his face in his paws.

'*Sewer* rats?' asked the field rat suspiciously.

Clarke sighed. 'Let me deal with this. Winston, this is Clarke. We're here to rescue you.'

Winston slowly turned to look at them, and his ear pricked up. 'Clarke?' he asked. 'Is it really you? I thought I was going to be here for ever and ever and the only way I'd be allowed out is if I had to go and live somewhere dark and strange like the sewers and NEVER SEE ZADIE AGAIN!'

Clarke pushed a paw through the bars of the cage and prodded Winston gently. 'That isn't happening. COBRA is here to rescue you. Now get up.'

'And quickly please,' hissed Coby. 'Harry could be back at any time.'

Mickey ran her hands over the cage and

found a large round padlock covering the door. She looked around the room but couldn't see a key.

Her brain quickly put a plan of action together. 'Let's not waste time. Clarke—go and fetch Bertie.'

Clarke glared at Mickey for a second, astounded that she would dare give him an order, before begrudgingly turning on his paws and racing back outside.

'Giraffes have such powerful kicks they can win fights against lions. If Bertie kicks the cage, he should be able to loosen the lock, and then we can rescue Winston. Winston—can you move towards the furthest edge of the cage and cover your eyes with your paws please?'

Winston quickly followed Mickey's instructions while Clarke led Bertie towards the cage. He had to bend almost double to fit inside the container, but when he saw the problem he nodded. 'Stand back,' he said to Mickey, who shuffled over to stand outside with Clarke and Coby. Bertie screwed up his face as he focused all his energy, and then he slammed his front right hoof into the hinge on the other side of the cage's door. It was no match for a giraffe. The hinge broke and the door fell forward.

'Come on, Winston,' Mickey urged, holding out her hand.

'I'm scared!' Winston trembled in the corner of his cage even though the door was open.

Suddenly there was a rustling sound, and Rupert's voice called into the container: 'The field rats say the human staff are coming this way.'

Mickey scrambled into the cage and grabbed Winston. Gripping him tightly, she carried him straight out of the container: followed by Clarke, Coby, and Bertie. They joined the others in the wooded area outside.

'Winston!' said Astrid. 'You're safe!'

Winston, who was overcome with emotion, let out a loud whimper. 'I'm so pleased to be free. Can you take me back to my Zadie? But safely—I don't want to be dognapped again!'

'We'll get you back as soon as possible,'

said Coby in the kindest voice Mickey had ever heard her use. 'But now that you're safe, we must recover the diamonds. And that means bringing in Harry.' Coby's eyes narrowed menacingly. 'Back to HQ.'

The animals and Mickey all looked at each other. Coby meant business.

'Right,' said Coby, addressing the **COBRA** members back at HQ. 'The good news is that Winston is back. The bad news is that Harry is still at large and in possession of the diamonds. He must be stopped!'

'It won't be easy. Harry has inside knowledge of **COBRA**—he can always be one step ahead,' reasoned Tilda.

'Not quite, Tilda,' Coby replied. 'Harry doesn't know *everything* about **COBRA**.' She looked directly at Mickey. 'We've been betrayed by a human once before, so I want you to think very carefully about the question I am about to ask you. Can we trust you Mickey?'

Mickey took a deep breath and met Coby's gaze.

'Yes,' she said firmly. 'And I won't rest until Harry is brought to justice.'

'I knew you were a good human!' Astrid yelled, flinging her arms around Mickey and landing a sloppy spider monkey kiss on her cheek.

Chapter
25

Mickey wondered if the receptionist would recognize her—she had been back to **The Grand Hotel** three times now—except this time, Clarke was hiding inside her backpack and Coby had curled herself around Mickey's neck, like a very thick and fancy scarf.

But Mickey made it through reception unnoticed and marched to **Room 103**. She knocked on the door, hoping this would be third time lucky and they would get the answers they needed.

Harry opened the door and gave an exasperated sigh when he saw Mickey.

'You again? I've told you this isn't your room. Now buzz off.' He went to close the door, but Mickey blocked it with her foot as Coby unravelled herself from Mickey's neck and slipped inside. Then Mickey stepped into the room and Clarke jumped out of the bag—

and the three **COBRA** members turned to face the runaway agent.

'Coby? Clarke?' said Harry with a smile, running a hand through his hair. 'It's been too long—who is your friend?'

Coby flared her hood furiously.

'We know you've been posing as "Mia" and blackmailing our friends and getting them to steal from their owners. And you dognapped Winston when he refused to help you. What do you have to say for yourself?'

The easy grin fell from Harry's face, and his eyes narrowed slightly. He clenched his fists and stalked across the room to sit on the desk by the window.

'Oh, you figured it out, did you?' he sneered. 'Took you long enough. But you're too late.'

Clarke hissed. All his fur seemed to be standing up in his rage.

'Where are the diamonds, Harry?' Coby demanded, with an air of quiet menace.

Harry gave a hollow laugh.

'I've worked too hard to have my plans

foiled by a snake, a cat, and some kid.'

Mickey bristled at this—she was not *some kid.*

'Well,' hissed Coby, looking scarier than Mickey had ever seen her. 'There are more of us than there are of you—and let's just say that some of us can be rather *persuasive* when we need to be.' The cobra slithered slowly towards Harry, then rose up to full height, her hood flaring, ready to attack.

Mickey darted over and opened the door to let in Rupert and the field rats who were waiting on the other side. They swarmed to surround Harry, baring their teeth and jumping up and down.

'You can't hide from us, Harry. Animals are everywhere, and we all have our eyes on you,' said Coby.

Mickey stepped forward to join the rats. 'Coby is right. Tell us where the diamonds are, and they won't harm you.'

The rats inched closer, and Coby swayed menacingly from side to side before drawing herself up to her tallest height and flashing her venomous fangs. Harry raised his arms and held his palms up in the air.

'Fine. Fine, you win. The diamonds are at Apartment 5B, Elgar Street. Now call off your pests.' He shot an angry glare at the field rats, who glared right back at him.

Coby settled back down, pleased with this new information. 'Thank you,' she told Harry. 'Of course, you'll understand if we don't entirely take your word for it, so if you'll accompany us to **COBRA** HQ while we check the address, we have a few more questions for you.'

'Oh, I don't think so,' said Harry, who had been fiddling with the window while Coby regrouped. 'I can't believe I wasted those years working with a bunch of useless animals like you lot. The only animal of any value in your organization was always Clarke, and I can't believe he's happy wasting his time with the rest of you.' Harry pulled himself out of the window, away from Coby and the field rats. Then he turned to address Clarke directly. 'What do you say, Clarkey?

Fancy a ticket to freedom and joining me instead? I'll make it worth your while.'

Mickey waited for Clarke's icy put-down, but none came. Clarke was silent and seemed to be deep in thought.

'Clarke,' Mickey whispered. 'You can't!'

Clarke turned to look at her with his wide green eyes. Then he swished his tail and stalked over to Harry.

'On the contrary, Mickey, I think you'll find that I can. I'm a good agent. Too good to have been tasked with babysitting a small human. At least Harry respects my skills and knows my true value. Harry, I accept your offer. Let's leave these idiots behind and find a place more suitable for those of our status.'

He took an elegant leap over the field rats to land on the desk and then sprang out of the window to join Harry. Mickey caught the horrible grin on Harry's face before, in a flash, he and Clarke were gone.

'TRAITOR!'
spat Coby.

Chapter 26

'The RAT!!' Coby was absolutely furious. Mickey had never seen her look so angry.

'Hey!' objected Rupert, and all the field rats looked terribly offended.

'She didn't mean it,' said Mickey quickly. 'She's just had a shock.'

If Coby'd had legs she would have been pacing up and down, but instead she was slithering furiously in a figure of eight.

'RIGHT,' she commanded . 'We may have been betrayed *by two of our own* now. But there is no time to lose. It's unlikely they're there, but we need to check Elgar Street RIGHT AWAY in case that *weasel* was telling the truth.'

Mickey ran faster than she'd ever run to try and keep up with the group as they bolted out of the hotel and through the city's streets until they reached Elgar Street. Number 5B did not look promising, it was covered in scaffolding and looked little more than a building site.

'That human seems to be in charge,' Coby hissed, pointing her tail at a man in a blue helmet. 'Go and ask him where 5B is.'

Mickey trudged over and called out, 'Hello! I was supposed to drop a letter round for 5B?'

The man looked at her, bewildered. 'Sorry, lass, you've either got the wrong address or you've missed them by a long way. This place has been derelict for ages—burned down years ago. We've been putting it back together for the last couple of months but still a long way to go until anyone can live here.'

'Yes, I must have got the address wrong,' said Mickey, walking back to where Coby and Rupert were eagerly waiting for news.

'Do you think Harry burned it down?' Rupert asked, when Mickey relayed their conversation.

'No, I think Coby was right and he did give us a fake address!' said Mickey.

'That ra—awful human!' said Coby,

avoiding Rupert's hurt glance.

Mickey couldn't believe it. Harry had tricked them. Now he had the diamonds *and* had turned Clarke to his side. What were they going to do now?

Mickey, Coby, and Rupert found Astrid consoling Winston when they returned to COBRA HQ.

'He's worried he'll be re-dognapped if he goes home,' said Astrid, seeing them coming in.

'Where's Clarke?' asked Tilda.

Coby just hissed and forced herself to focus on Winston.

'**COBRA** will protect you. We'll make sure you are safe.'

'Indeed we will,' said Rupert. 'The field rats have formed a perimeter around your house and they will notify us of anything suspicious.'

'Plus, I don't think Zadie is going to let you out of her sight once she gets you back,' said Astrid. 'And we got you back before a ransom was issued, so she might just think you wandered off.'

Winston's eyes lit up at the thought of Zadie. 'That was good work! I don't want to worry her, and I do want to see her, but,' his front paws began to tremble, 'OH I'M SCARED!'

Mickey came forward and rested one hand on his golden ears. 'I know it's scary, but we'll keep you safe, I promise.'

Winston leaned into Mickey and licked her hand. 'You have been very kind,' he said.

'Can I go home please?' he asked. 'I do miss Zadie so!'

Mickey looked to Coby, who nodded sharply.

Mickey phoned the number on Winston's collar with Astrid hanging over her shoulder so that she could listen in. It rang once then a gruff voice answered.

'Hello?'

'Hello,' said Mickey politely. 'I found a dog in the park, and I think he belongs to you.'

'What's he look like?' the man continued, as Mickey heard Zadie's voice in the background: 'Oh! Has someone found Winston? Is he okay? Can I see him?!'

'He's a golden spaniel and has a collar with a pattern of dog bones on it.'

'That's him, that's him!' she heard Zadie squealing in the background.

The male voice continued to show little emotion. 'If you take him to your nearest vet's, we can arrange collection from there—which is your local?'

Mickey racked her brain to remember

if she'd seen a veterinary practice near
COBRA HQ.

'Alasdair James—Veterinary Surgeon,'
Astrid whispered in her ear.

'Alasdair James—Veterinary Surgeon,'
Mickey repeated.

'Very good,' said the voice. 'Thank you for
phoning.'

'Winston,' said Coby. 'I'm pleased you're
back safe; we'll be in touch should we need
anything else from you.'

'Of course,' said Winston politely. 'My
sincere thanks for your help. And Mickey, I'm
sorry for not trusting you at the start. I shan't
make that mistake again.'

Mickey smiled and picked Winston up into
her arms because he was trembling so much
from a mixture of nerves and excitement that
she was worried he might not be able to walk.
He was quite a heavy dog, and she staggered
slightly under his weight, but together
with Astrid, who quietly called directions
over Mickey's shoulder, she managed to
get Winston over to Alasdair James—

Veterinary Surgeon.

As soon as they arrived at the vet's, Zadie came hurtling out of the back office.

'Oh WINSTON!' she cried, scooping him up.

Winston's tail wagged so fast it became a blur as he joyfully woofed and licked Zadie all over her face.

'Where have you been?' she cried out. In his excitement Winston began to answer, but Mickey only caught 'You'll never guess . . .' before Zadie smothered him in kisses.

Mickey couldn't believe Zadie was standing right in front of her and suddenly found she couldn't think of anything to say, so she leaned quietly against the wall and watched Zadie and Winston's joyful reunion.

Then Zadie, with Winston held tight in one arm, swept the other arm around Mickey, covering her

in a cloud of perfume.

'How can I ever thank you?' she asked, turning to Mickey.

'I'm just glad he's back safely. He's a lovely dog,' said Mickey shyly.

'Oh, he is just the *best*!' said Zadie happily. 'You wouldn't believe how much I've missed him! Well, we need to do something to say thank you! You *must* come to my next concert. We'll get you a box—the full VIP treatment for you and all your friends.'

She gestured to one of the security guards, who came over and took down Mickey's address in a little blue notebook. Then Zadie buried her face in the dog's fur and Mickey felt a feeling of pride spread through her whole body.

But the diamonds were still missing. And then there were Harry and Clarke to deal with. Mickey winced. She had thought that Clarke was growing to respect her. She must have been mistaken, and the truth hurt.

Chapter
27

COBRA was thrown into complete disarray by Clarke's betrayal. Mickey hadn't heard from them for over a week apart from a Bird-Mail from Astrid to say things were not going well at the HQ—'venom everywhere' she'd said— and she advised Mickey to give Coby a wide berth until things had calmed down.

Mickey found the sudden change back to normal life jarring when compared to the excitement of running around the city with a gang of animal spies. She followed several black cats, but none of them turned out to be Clarke. She was still carrying her spy kit around with her, though she had no occasion to use it.

The following weekend, Mickey took herself off to a quiet bench in the park, flung her spy kit on the ground, sat herself down, and frowned.

Thoughts of **COBRA** kept pinging into her mind. When would it be safe to return to HQ? Did they have any leads on Harry or Clarke? And just what was that rustling sound above her head?

The rustling grew louder, and then a small robin shot out of the tree and landed right on top of Mickey's spy kit. It looked from side to side then carefully swept its wing up to its head and tapped three times, its eyes fixed on Mickey's.

Mickey's heart leapt! She held the robin's gaze and blinked slowly, three times.

The robin gave a soft cheep and flew on to Mickey's shoulder.

'What's your name?' asked the bird quietly.

'Michaela Rose Thompson,' she replied. 'But everyone calls me Mickey.'

'Oh PHEW!' said the little bird. 'I found you. I have a Bird-Mail for you from Clarke.'

CLARKE?? Mickey thought, but she did her best to keep her cool. 'What does it say?' she asked calmly.

The bird hopped up and down with

excitement. 'You were really hard to find. He
said to look for a small, determined human with
a backpack who knew the **COBRA** greeting. It's a
parcel service. He said to give you this.' The bird
cheeped, and a second robin shot down from the
tree with a piece of paper held carefully in its
beak. It landed next to Mickey and carefully set
the paper down next to her.

'Message delivered safely,' cheeped the small bird.

Mickey examined the piece of paper. There was a dent in the middle from the robin's beak, but she unfolded it gently, wondering what Clarke could have sent her. To her surprise she saw it was a code.

M—OBVIOUSLY HARRY GAVE
A FAKE ADDRESS.
THE REAL ADDRESS IS
17 CARAWAY AVENUE.
COME QUICKLY—C

She tried not to get her hopes up—it would be just like Clarke to send her a rude message in code—but Hildegarde would never leave a code unsolved, and neither would Mickey. She just needed to work out how to solve it.

Chapter 28

Try as she might, Mickey couldn't make head nor tail of Clarke's message. She suspected it was made more difficult by the fact the letter had been written by a cat, so didn't contain the usual letter shapes she was used to. She wondered if it was ancient runes, but the symbols didn't match up. Then she tried counting the number of lines in each symbol to see if it was a numerical code, but it wasn't. Mickey moved her eyes up and down and from left to right but the solution stubbornly refused to click into place.

She then heard the joyful barking of a dog, whose human had let it go in the muddiest part of the park, and who was now bounding around the edge of the lake and getting all wet. The parts of the park lake that weren't being disturbed by the dog were so clear that Mickey could see the clouds reflecting perfectly in the water.

The observation stuck in her brain—*reflecting*.

Quickly she picked up her spy kit from the ground and dug through it until she found her wallet and inside that—her mirror. She held it straight up to Clarke's message, and suddenly it began to make sense.

M – OBVIOUSLY HARRY
GAVE
A FAKE ADDRESS.
THE REAL ADDRESS IS
17 CARAWAY AVENUE.
COME QUICKLY – C

There was not a second to waste. Mickey addressed the patiently waiting robin: 'Please can I send a Bird-Mail to COBRA HQ? Can you tell them that Clarke's asked me to come to 17 Caraway Avenue, and I'm going there to investigate?'

The robin shot off as Mickey
stood up and slung her spy kit over
her shoulders. She didn't know
whether to trust Clarke, but
there was only one
thing to do—
walk *towards*
the puzzle, not
away from it. She
was going to
Caraway
Avenue!

Chapter
29

Caraway Avenue consisted of a series of holiday apartments across town. They were slightly run-down and shabby looking—worlds away from Harry's room at **The Grand Hotel**.

Mickey tiptoed up to number 17 and noticed the door slightly ajar. With the sound of her heart pumping loudly in her ears, she pushed the door and came face to face with Clarke's green eyes staring straight at her.

'What took you so long?' he said huffily.

Mickey glared at him. 'That's rich coming from you! You're the one who betrayed COBRA and went off with Harry. You're lucky I decided to come at all. Why on earth should I trust you?'

The cat's face softened in a way that Mickey hadn't seen before. 'Because I tell the truth, and I also know a liar when I see one. I knew Harry had given you a fake address, and so

I decided to pretend to be on his side to find out the real address. It was always my plan to let **COBRA** know the location.'

'So why not go direct to Coby?' asked Mickey.

'I figured that she might not be quite ready to hear from me yet . . .' Clarke looked sheepish. 'Anyway, if I *was* going to switch sides, it wouldn't be with that oaf Harry. He always did underestimate animals. He wanted to lie low while things settled, and he wouldn't leave me on my own or I'd have called you earlier. But finally he had to go out for supplies, so I sent you a message in code to be on the safe side. You may be just a small human, but you *are* good at solving puzzles.'

Mickey had a brief moment to take in the fact that a) Clarke hadn't actually betrayed **COBRA** and b) he had just paid her another compliment. She couldn't help smiling.

'Hurry up and help me look for the diamonds,' Clarke continued. 'He'll be back soon so we have to be quick and I need your thumbs.'

Mickey stepped inside. At first glance there didn't seem to be anywhere obvious to hide the diamonds, but she'd read enough detective stories to know to knock for hollow walls and to check the floorboards for any loose ones that could be concealing a secret space. Together she and Clarke worked their way around the room, but no hiding place revealed itself.

Next they tried the living room and shower room—no luck.

Then the two bedrooms, taking one each.

'Nothing in my room,' she called.

'Nor mine,' Clarke replied, meeting her back in the hall.

The last room was the kitchen, which was painted such a bright yellow that Mickey felt like she should be wearing sunglasses.

Quickly, she rummaged through the cupboards, which were packed with tins of sardines and nothing else. 'There's nothing here but tins of fish!' she called to Clarke, who had been inspecting the rest of the room.

He paused a moment, his whiskers twitching at the mention of fish, before he nodded.

'Nothing here either,' he reported.

'This is the last room. They have to be in here,' said Mickey.

'Or they could be somewhere else,' the cat replied glumly.

'We'll have to go back to **COBRA** and give them the information, so they can decide what to do next,' said Mickey.

There was a quiet moment, while both human and cat felt the sinking disappointment of realizing they wouldn't be able to triumphantly carry the diamonds back to **COBRA** HQ.

'All we really have to report is that they seem to like sardines an awful lot. Maybe that's how Harry got so clever—' As she said this, a piece of the puzzle clicked into place. 'Hang on.' Mickey jumped up and rummaged through the cupboard again, shaking tin after tin of sardines and then throwing them down on to the floor. Clarke yelped when they came too close to his paws, and he leapt up on to the counter.

'What are you doing?'

'No one could like sardines this much,' she said. 'And the best place to hide something is among lots of things that look the same.'

Clarke opened his mouth to respond, but then Mickey shook the next two tins and instead of the usual sloshing sound of sardines rolling around in oil, they heard a very clear 'clunk'.

'Sardines don't go "clunk"!' yelped Mickey. 'I think we've found them.'

She grabbed the ring pull of a tin and gently levered off the lid. Clarke peered over her shoulders, his jaw dropping at what Mickey was tipping out of the tin and into her hand.

'We found them!' she cried, just as the front door swung open and Coby, Rupert, and Astrid flew through with Tilda puffing along a few paces behind. 'We found the diamonds!'

Chapter
30

'Do you think she'll ever forgive me?' Clarke
asked Mickey seriously, as they sat in the
COBRA briefing room waiting for Coby and
the others to enter.

'Well . . . she was very angry when you left
with Harry,' Mickey said.

'I was only pretending,' said Clarke. 'And
we did get the diamonds back.'

'That's true,' said Mickey, clocking his use
of the word 'we' rather than him taking all
the credit as he usually did. 'I think Coby's as
pleased about that as she was cross when you
switched sides, so maybe it all balances out?'

Just then the door swung open and Coby,
Rupert and Astrid entered to take their seats,
then sat patiently while Tilda made her own
slow motion entrance.

'Greetings,' said Coby. 'Thanks to excellent
work by Mickey and Clarke, who has turned

out *not to be a traitor,* we have successfully retrieved the stolen diamonds. All animals across all **COBRA** operations have been briefed and have been tasked with finding Harry. It's proving difficult, as he may be in disguise again, but it's only a matter of time until we catch that double-crossing human!'

'Are all the diamonds safely back with the correct humans?' asked Tilda, who liked all loose ends to be tied up satisfactorily.

'They are,' said Coby. 'Max, Ruby, and Thor all send their thanks. The field rats returned all the jewels to their rightful owners— and apparently the humans are all utterly perplexed, though happy of course to have their precious jewels back. I therefore declare Operation Shiny Dog closed,' she announced. 'We should celebrate.'

'Oh, do we have to? groaned Tilda.

'Why don't you like to celebrate?' asked Mickey.

'Coby likes to celebrate by lying in a hot room,' explained Astrid. 'Which is much less pleasant if you have fur.'

'It does get rather
uncomfortable,' added Rupert,
stroking his whiskers nervously.

'I've got an idea,' said Mickey. 'Zadie gave
me some tickets to her concert. Why don't we
make that a celebration?'

'Hmm,' said Clarke. 'That sounds like quite
a *human* way of celebrating, and won't we
be seen?'

'They're for a VIP box, so it's quite private,'
said Mickey. 'And there will be free food.'

'I think this sounds excellent,' said
Rupert immediately.

'Me too!' agreed Astrid.

'Fine,' said Coby, flicking her tail.
'Mickey—that is a generous offer and
we accept.'

Chapter

31

Mickey told her parents she was going to Zadie's concert with some friends and darted out of the flat wearing her mum's long, red trench coat and her own favourite boots, which she'd polished until they shone. She met up with the **COBRA** High Committee outside the venue, and everyone hid under the coat. Bertie was too big to fit, so Mickey draped him in his own trench coat, a hat, and a very, very long scarf. Together they moved carefully past the human security guards, pretending to be two normal people looking forward to the concert, rather than one human, a rat, a cat, a spider monkey, a cobra, a sloth, and a giraffe.

Once inside, Mickey navigated their way up to the VIP box that Zadie had arranged for her. It was like having their own mini living room to watch the concert from. There

were several low couches, a table
heaving with cakes, pastries,
strawberry tarts, and fruit—

and the perfect view of the stage, which was
set for Zadie's performance.

Mickey loosened her coat, and the animal
spies came out of hiding and stretched their
limbs awkwardly.

'Grapes!' cried Astrid, launching herself at the fruit platter.

Mickey leaned over to help Rupert, who was using his teeth to try to untie the knot in Bertie's scarf. Coby slithered straight over to the balcony to see what exactly was on the other side, while Clarke jumped from seat to seat trying to work out which one was the comfiest.

'Where's Tilda?' he asked, as he found one he liked and stretched himself out.

'She's just napping,' replied Mickey, who could see that Tilda had made a beeline straight for the darkest corner of the room and was now fast asleep. 'This is brilliant!' Mickey ran over to join Coby at the balcony and looked down to see thousands of Zadie's fans holding glow sticks that shone in the darkness of the auditorium. The background music was sending a beat through the whole building, and spotlights were sending shimmering colours all around the room.

Then suddenly there was a knock at the door and a voice said, 'Mickey?' Mickey knew that voice—it was Zadie!

'Quick, hide!' she whispered loudly to the animals. In a flash, Clarke was out of his seat and tucked underneath it. Coby slithered out from the balcony railing and hung down out of sight, her tail gripping the railing tightly. Astrid and Rupert ran to the corner to keep Tilda quiet, in case she suddenly woke up, and Mickey quickly threw her red coat over Bertie, who folded his long legs down and tried to tuck himself into the wall.

Mickey gave the room a quick sweep, and when she was satisfied they were hidden she threw open the door.

'Zadie!' she cried happily.

'Ah. I'm so pleased you could come!' said Zadie, swooping her arms around Mickey in a hug. 'And Winston wanted to see you too.'

Behind Zadie, Winston barked happily and then padded over to nuzzle against Mickey's leg.

'I'm not letting him out of my sight after what happened. If it wasn't for you I don't know what I'd have done! And I'm so pleased you could make the show. Are you enjoying the box?'

'It's wonderful,' said Mickey, suddenly feeling shy again in front of the sparkly pop star.

'And is this your friend?' asked Zadie, who had spotted Bertie and was moving towards him with her arms outstretched for a hug.

'Yes . . .' said Mickey, alarmed. 'But he's very . . . superstitious. He thinks it's bad luck to see you before the performance.'

A hint of a frown wrinkled across Zadie's face.

'And he's very shy.' Mickey grabbed Zadie's hand to lead her away from Bertie. 'This is SO kind of you,' she said as they leaned over the box balcony. 'The view is amazing!'

Zadie looked down at all the people waiting for her and took a deep breath. 'I should probably get down there! I'm on soon. Enjoy the show, and thanks *so* much for coming.' She kissed Mickey on both cheeks, and then in a cloud of perfume she was gone.

'Can I stand up now?' asked Bertie desperately.

'Yes, yes, the coast is clear!' said Mickey.

'Urrrrgh,' said the giraffe, as he shook the coat off and stretched himself up to his full height. 'My neck is all pins and needles!'

At this point, Coby slithered back in from the balcony, just as Rupert, Tilda, Astrid, and Clarke each claimed their spots on the couches.

'That was very well handled, Mickey,' said Coby. 'And we have one more question to ask of you, and this seems as good a time as any. We may have doubted your abilities when you first arrived, but over the course of Operation Shiny Dog you have proven yourself more than worthy of the ranks of COBRA. We like how your brain works, how you conduct yourself, and your willingness to seek out the truth, no matter what. And so we would like to officially offer you the post of COBRA's Human Liaison Officer—if you are still interested. Do you think it's a role you might be interested in, going forward?'

Mickey thought of hiding in the alley that stank of fish, and the dreadful feeling when no one would believe her about Ruby. But then she thought of the joy of cracking codes, the happiness of investigating with an animal riding on her back, the relief of freeing Winston, and the satisfaction of returning the diamonds to their rightful owners. Best of all, though, there was having a haughty cat, a friendly spider monkey, a dignified rat, a plodding sloth, a large giraffe, and, of course, a slightly scary cobra as friends. There was only one answer she could give.

'Of course!' she replied. 'Count me in!'

'Oh, I'm so pleased you said yes!' cried Astrid.

'Welcome aboard, my dear,' said Rupert.

'I knew she'd say yes,' said Clarke dismissively, but when Mickey caught his eye he winked.

Then the High Committee of COBRA, plus their brand-new Human Liaison Officer sat together eating strawberry tarts. They watched the lights swirl around the room as

the music dimmed and joined in
with the roar of the audience as
Zadie appeared on the stage—
chandelier earrings in place, and
holding a silver microphone.

While the others were transfixed by
what was happening onstage, Mickey
looked around at her new friends and
colleagues. She was the happiest she had
ever been. And she couldn't wait to see
what happened next.

DID YOU SPOT THE MAGNIFYING GLASS CODE
AT THE BEGINNING OF EACH CHAPTER?

Animal Alphabet Code

A	🐵	J	🦊	S	🐌
B	🐰	K	🐨	T	🐯
C	🦉	L	🐭	U	🐴
D	🦘	M	🐁	V	🐥
E	🐘	N	🐐	W	🦭
F	🐱	O	🐙	X	🐤
G	🦒	P	🐧	Y	🦛
H	🦔	Q	🐝	Z	🦓
I	🐞	R	🦌		

About the author

Anne Miller grew up
in Scotland and now
lives in London
where she makes TV
and radio programmes
including BBC Two's
QI and Radio Four's
*The Museum of
Curiosity*. She reached
the semi-finals of the fiendishly
difficult quiz show *Only Connect* and
has two *Blue Peter* badges. Her current
favourite animal is a Golden Retriever.

ANNE MILLER

About the illustrator

BECKA MOOR

Becka Moor is a
children's book
illustrator living in
Manchester. She studied
illustration for
children's publishing
at Glyndwr University,
graduating in 2012.
Since then, she has
worked on a variety
of young fiction,
non-fiction & picture books. She has
a slight obsession with cats and likes
anything a bit on the quirky side.

Number Replacement Code

```
3-12-1-18-11-5'19
13-9-4-4-12-5
14-1-13-5  9-19
13-15-14-20-1-7-21-5
```

A	B	C	D	E	F	G	H	I	J	K	L	M
1	2	3	4	5	6	7	8	9	10	11	12	13

N	O	P	Q	R	S	T	U	V	W	X	Y	Z
14	15	16	17	18	19	20	21	22	23	24	25	26

Mirror Quiz

1. What is the capital city of France?

2. What do you call a female sheep?

3. What is the name for a bad dream?

4. What colour do you get if you mix blue and yellow paint?

5. What is the opposite of down?

6. What does water turn into when it is frozen?

7. What is the name of the eighth planet from the sun?

8. Which animal is spelled out by the first letters of all your previous answers?

....

Bonus point if you can write your answer in mirror writing:

....

Note from Mickey
If you use capital letters, some are easier to do in mirror writing than others.
A, H, I, M, O, T, U, V, W, X, and Y are the same as the usual way, but letters like F, R, and Z are harder!

F R Z | Z R F

(ANSWERS: 1. PARIS 2. EWE 3. NIGHTMARE 4. GREEN 5. UP 6. ICE 7. NEPTUNE 8. PENGUIN)

A huge thank you to my Mum and Dad, to Alasdair and to Sam for more than I can say.

A signature Coby tailshake to my (Secret) Agent Louise Lamont for immeasurable wisdom and loving books the way I do.

To everyone at OUP for embracing the world of animal spies. Special Field Rat Salutes to Clare Whitston, Gillian Sore, Hannah Penny, Liz Scott, Kate Penrose, Emily Thomas and Laura Baker.

To Becka Moor for her incredible illustrations. Clarke hopes his request that he be drawn at twice the size of everyone else be heeded in book two.

Thank you to Sarah Lloyd, John Lloyd and everyone at QI and Museum for making life quite interesting. And to Team Standard Issue for giving me my first home to write about books.

Huge Astrid hugs to Robin Stevens for being endlessly supportive and reading early drafts, to David Stevens and Anna James for being there from the start and to Ben, Sara, Mira, Adam, Cynthia, James, Jay and Joe for everything.

And to good dogs and furious cats everywhere and to Sam (again!) for always helping me spot them.

ANNE MILLER